THE JUNIOR NOVELIZATION

TITAN A.E. TM & © 2000 Twentieth Century Fox Film Corporation.
All rights reserved. Published by Price Stern Sloan, a division of Penguin
Putnam Books for Young Readers, New York. PSS! is a registered trademark of
Penguin Putnam Inc. Published simultaneously in Canada.
Printed in the U.S.A.
Library of Congress Catalog Number: 00-132560
ISBN 0-8431-7584-2   A B C D E F G H I J

TITAN A.E.™

THE JUNIOR NOVELIZATION

Adapted by C. R. Daly

PSS!
PRICE STERN SLOAN

CHAPTER 1

Five-year-old Cale Tucker crouched next to a bubbling stream. His brow wrinkled in concentration, he carefully placed his creation into the water. The cleverly made toy bobbed, righted itself, and merrily made its way downstream.

"Perfect," said Cale.

Suddenly, the toy began racing down the stream, out of control.

"Hey!" called Cale. "Stop… come on!" He stood up and raced after it. Crash! Cale tumbled to the ground. Looking up, he saw that he was lying at the feet of his father, Sam Tucker. Sam's handsome face looked pensive. He held Cale's toy in his hand.

"Dad, my invention broke," Cale said sadly.

Sam silently reached down and lifted up his son. He looked thoughtfully at Cale for a moment, then ran his hand gently along the boy's face. The ring on Sam's finger glinted in the blazing noon sun.

"Later, Cale," said Sam. "We have to go now." He turned and started walking up a hill. Over his father's shoulder, Cale stared unhappily at the stream.

When they reached the top of the hill, Sam stopped for a moment to survey the valley below. The scene was one of utter chaos. Rockets streaked across the sky. The valley was packed full of thousands upon thousands of rocket ships. Humans and aliens alike swarmed around each one, desperate to get on board. Military officers were trying to control the crowds, but it was nearly impossible. Cale watched in wonder as one of the ships took off, shooting straight into the sky. The people below looked panicked, desperate. It scared him a little. What was going on? "Dad, where's everybody going?" he asked.

Sam sighed. "I wish we knew," he said. "We all have to go somewhere safe." Deep in thought, he stared at the frantic hordes of people.

A voice interrupted his thoughts. "Professor Tucker! Professor Tucker!" Sam looked up. A hover jeep was heading toward them. A tough-looking young officer named Korso was driving. A large, friendly-looking alien with yellow eyes named Tek was in the passenger seat. The jeep came to a stop, floating in mid-air. "Professor Tucker!" Tek said again. "The Drej have breached the global defense system!"

Sam looked worried. "Will we get the people away in time?" he asked.

"Not if we sit here talking, sir," snapped Korso.

Quickly, Sam hoisted Cale into the jeep and hopped in beside him. Cale looked at the jeep appreciatively. "I wanna drive!" he announced.

Korso gave him a quick glance over his shoulder. "When you're older, kid," he said.

"I'm older than four," said Cale with childlike logic.

"Hang on!" shouted Korso. The hover jeep took off with a lurch.

Sam leaned over and asked Tek, "Is the *Titan* prepped for launch?"

"Just waiting for you, sir!" said Tek.

"Intelligence says the Drej don't know about the *Titan* or else we would have been hit already," explained Korso.

"Let's pray that they're right," said Sam.

While the adults talked about things he didn't understand, Cale scanned the sky, watching the rockets streak across the horizon. Weird things were going on today. Everyone seemed to have this sense of urgency. Why wasn't anyone telling him anything? Cale sighed. He knew—it was because he was a kid. Adults always tried to keep important things from kids.

Korso drove the hover jeep off the cliff. It glided smoothly to the ground, and Korso steered it expertly through the crowds of desperate men, women, children, and aliens. He pulled up alongside one of the rocket ships.

Cale stared, his mouth open. Cool! He had always wanted to ride in one of these! "Are we going in *that*?" he asked. "Wow!"

Sam hopped out of the jeep and lifted his son out. Placing Cale gently on the ground, he knelt next to him and looked deeply into his eyes. Cale stared at his father, fear mounting in his heart. Something was wrong—very wrong. He had a feeling he didn't to want to hear what his father was about to say.

"Cale," Sam began softly, "I have to go on a different ship. I have to go away for a while."

Cale stared at his father in disbelief. This was worse than he could have imagined! "No, Dad!" he shouted. "No!"

"Tek is going to look after you," his father explained.

But Cale would hear none of it. "I want to go with you!" he wailed.

Sam bit his lip. "I know. But it's not safe where I'm going."

"I don't care," said Cale stubbornly.

"Professor," Korso interrupted. Time was running out!

Sam looked over his shoulder. "All right! I'm coming!" he shouted, and grasped the ring on his finger. "Cale, here, take this," he said, placing it on his son's finger. Cale watched, transfixed, as the ring magically re-sized itself to fit his small finger.

"I want you to always keep this," Sam said solemnly. "I will see you again, okay?"

Cale looked at the ring, then at his father's saddened face. "Okay," he whispered.

Sam turned to go. Cale couldn't stand it. His father couldn't leave! Cale lunged forward and grabbed Sam's leg, hanging on for dear life.

"No, it's not okay! It's not okay!" Cale howled. The agony in his voice made Sam wince in pain.

Sam picked up the boy and held him tight. But time was running out. He had to go. "Cale, now you mind Tek!" he said. He kissed his son gently on the forehead. Then, his heart breaking, he handed his only son to his alien friend and jumped back into the jeep.

"Daddy!" wailed Cale.

Sam couldn't turn around and face his son.

"Come back!" Cale cried, his heart breaking.

Blocking out his son's cries, Sam motioned for Korso to take off. They zoomed across the field to a huge silo. Sam gripped Korso's shoulder briefly, jumped out of the jeep, and pulled out a walkie-talkie. "This is Tucker. Bring me down!"

The silo doors slid open, revealing a metal platform. A disembodied female voice issued a warning: "Attention pilots, Drej stingers are attacking the escape route." Sam stepped onto the platform and it began to lower.

Back on the tarmac, Tek put his arm around the heartbroken boy and shepherded him onto one of the rocket ships. One by one, each of the remaining ships blasted off. With a great roar, their ship fired to life. It shuddered as it began to rise into the sky. As the smoke below the ship cleared, Tek and Cale watched, transfixed, as several Drej stingers appeared out of nowhere, firing their weapons. They weren't leaving a moment too soon.

The boy and the alien pressed their faces against the window. Sam's ship still had not taken off. What was the delay? Time was running out! Far below them, in the empty landing area, massive sliding doors started to part. Would Sam make it in time? Cale watched, his heart pounding. Where was the ship his father spoke of? Where was his father? "Now, Sam, now! Get out of there! Get out of there!" Tek whispered under his breath.

Cale and Tek stared out the window, scarcely daring to breathe. The same thought that neither dared to speak was on both their minds: What if Sam didn't make it?

Suddenly, an enormous gleaming sphere emerged from the open doors. It was the *Titan*, the greatest invention humankind had ever created. The ship paused for a moment. Neither Tek nor Cale could take their eyes off it. It was huge. It was powerful. It was beautiful. Then, as they watched, its four powerful thrusters blasted the *Titan* into space. The two looked at each other with relief written on their faces. Sam was safe—for now. So there was hope after all.

As Cale and Tek watched the *Titan's* daring escape, they were unaware that a monstrous ship loomed in the distance. It was the Drej mothership. It seemed to suck up all the light around it. The Drej queen, the central intelligence that drove the entire Drej race, barked out orders to her unseen minions. Her face was dark and evil. Her power was so great that she was less a person than a force of brilliant light and shadow. "Now we finish it," she hissed.

The mothership aimed a glowing beam of cold blue light at the North Pole. Within seconds, bright blue stripes of light blanketed the entire planet. The Earth began to spin faster and faster. Then, a web of cracks appeared on the Earth's surface, and it began to crumble, a deep cleft running through the middle of the planet. Cale watched through unbelieving eyes as the crust of his home planet bulged and the mantle sizzled. Then, able to take the pressure no more, the blue planet exploded, her tectonic plates bursting in a detonation of ribbons of magma and gas. The explosion was mercilessly loud. The moon, hit by debris, shattered.

The Drej mothership pulled away. Her job was done.

The Earth was gone.

CHAPTER 2

The lean twenty-year-old floated in space, concentrating as he deftly sliced through a huge section of steel. Despite the bulky spacesuit, he moved around quite easily. The young man worked with a cocky swagger, an attitude he created to shield the pain and loneliness he felt inside. It was a loneliness that could come only from losing a parent at a young age. It was Cale Tucker, fifteen years later.

Cale was busy working on salvaging a massive space ship. He finished cutting. In zero-G, he was able to push the huge piece of steel effortlessly out of the way. Po, an alien operating a space crane, picked up the piece and headed off with it, smacking Cale in the back of the helmet and knocking him down. Cale was furious! He picked up his laser torch and shot at the crane. "I'll get you!" Cale said angrily.

Cale's stomach grumbled. It must be close to lunchtime. He looked around at the other workers. In the dark sky, their torches glowed like the lights of fireflies. He grinned ruefully. It had been a long, long time since he had thought about fireflies. He could only vaguely remember them from his life on Earth, long ago. A walk through a field on a starry night, his father's hand clutching his …He shook his head to dislodge the memories. That was then and this was now. No sense in thinking about the past. His stomach grumbled again. Was it time for lunch yet?

Finally, the lunch bell rang. "One hour for lunch!" yelled Chowquin, the foreman. Alien and human workers alike dropped their equipment and hopped on their fire-powered scooters and headed toward the elevator. Chowquin checked their names off the list on his clipboard. The aliens crowded to the front, and a small group of humans waited silently behind them. Humans were definitely second-class citizens on this world.

Cale hopped onto his scooter and zipped through the space debris at breakneck speed, narrowly missing each one. No question about it—Cale was a daredevil. He zipped onto the line, just cutting someone off. Cale hated waiting, so he slipped in with the aliens. He shot into the air and repositioned himself in line, bumping into several angry aliens in the process. Chowquin held out his massive hand, barring the way.

A huge alien named Firrikash turned around angrily. "Hey!" he said.

Cale ignored him. "How ya hittin' 'em, Chowquin?" he asked. Time was wasting. Cale wanted inside—now.

"Wait," said the foreman.

"Chowquin, hey it's me," he said. "It's Cale, all right? I'm not with those *losers*," he said, motioning back to the humans who huddled together in the background.

But Chowquin would hear none of it. "Humans wait," he said, reaching out his huge hand, and effortlessly sending Cale flying back into the group of humans like a bowling ball.

The other humans laughed. "Guess you're stuck with us losers," one of them said.

Cale smirked. Him, a loser? "Well, don't count on it," he said. "You wait in line, pal," he sneered. "I'm taking the express."

Cale shot straight up into the air and headed toward the docking bays—and a shortcut. "Go through those docks and you'll get yourself killed!" the human yelled after him.

Cale laughed. "Coward!" he scoffed. "The odds of a ship docking are a thousand to one!" He looked up to see a massive ship pulling in, just a few feet away from him. He gasped. "And that would be the one. Whoa—oh!"

The huge shining ship that was just about to squash Cale was called the *Valkyrie*. The ship's nose hit him, crushed his scooter, and sent him reeling into space. Cale tumbled head over feet until his gravity boots landed him on the side of the massive ship. He crawled to the windshield of the ship, hoping to see who had sent him flying. Peering into the bridge, he could barely make out the lit dials and instruments. Wait—he could see someone. A human—make that a *female* human—make that a very *attractive* female human—was sitting in the pilot's chair. "Wow," said Cale. Things were definitely getting a little more interesting around here! Cale leaned forward to get a closer look and accidentally banged his head against the windshield.

Akima, the attractive female human, looked up sharply from the shutdown check she was conducting. Akima was only eighteen years old, but she was an expert pilot. She brushed a strand of purple hair out of her face and focused suspiciously on Cale. Cale smiled nonchalantly and pulled a rag from his pocket to wipe the windshield. He nodded pleasantly at her and whistled a merry tune as he cleaned.

Who was this arrogant—yet attractive—young man? Akima wondered. She stared back at him, her eyes narrowed, then she flicked a switch. Suddenly, steel blast shields began to close over the windshield.

"Hey!" Cale said in surprise. He thought things had been going pretty well!

As the shields were just about to slam shut, Cale jumped backwards. "Hey!" he shouted again. Akima smiled. Served him right! Then she turned around and said, "We're locked down, Captain."

The captain checked his gun and slipped it into his holster. "All right," he said. "Keep her hot. I'll be in touch." The door slid open and the captain paused for a moment before he stepped off the bridge.

• • •

Cale stood on the commissary line. What slop would they be serving today? The cook, who most unfortunately resembled a huge cockroach with a chef's hat perched on its head, rattled on as he dished out platefuls of what vaguely resembled spaghetti and meatballs. "How ya doin' today?" he said. "Working hard are you? Bon apetite. Keep the line moving. Here ya go!"

Cale held out his tray for a plateful of "lunch." His stomach lurched as the food squirmed around on his dish. He looked up at the cook.

"Got ketchup?" he asked.

The cook exploded. What an insult! "Ketchup? Ketchup! You don't need ketchup! Please! Next! Move along!" He angrily swiped at Cale with his serving spoon. Cale ducked.

Cale shrugged and walked into the dining room, scanning the crowd. A vast sea of strange alien faces stared back at him, not a friendly-looking one in the bunch. Finally, he spotted Tek and dropped down into the seat opposite him. He put a plateful of food in front of his alien friend and immediately started complaining. "You know," Cale began, "I'm not asking that much. I'd just like them to kill my food before they serve it to me." One of his meatballs squealed and bounced across the table. Cale caught it neatly in one hand and put it back on his plate. "You know, I do an honest day's work. I want already dead food. Is that too much for a fella to ask?"

But Tek wasn't paying attention. "Do you hear a crackling sound?" he asked, cocking his head.

Cale wasn't listening to him either. "And what was up with Chowquin?" he mused. "You should have seen him."

"Not much chance of that …" Tek said with a chuckle. He had since lost his ability to see.

Cale kept going. "He was so out of control. Treating me like I'm some kind of ..."

"Human?" said Tek.

Cale scowled at him. "Don't start with that solidarity thing again," he said with a groan.

Tek leaned forward. "If you would study your human history as you'd been instructed, you might realize you're not alone out there—and you'd be better prepared for the future."

But Cale had heard this story before. He sank down into his chair. "Well, I'll tell you something about your famous future," he said, twirling his fork in his spaghetti. "Everyday I wake up, it's still the present. The same grimy, boring present. I don't even think this 'future' thing exists." He paused for a moment, listening. "Do you hear a crackling sound?"

He turned around and took a long look at the gravity drive. There were wires dangling dangerously from the box, like a socket with too many extensions plugged into it. It crackled again. Then there was a big pop. Sparks rained down and an alarm started to blare. Cale shook his head. "Here we go..." he said.

Suddenly there was no longer any gravity. Everything that wasn't nailed down started to float. Plates, forks, and knives seemed to take on a life of their own. Aliens and humans in mid-step suddenly found themselves floating halfway up to the ceiling. Everyone started to panic. Only Cale and Tek stayed calm. They floated a few inches above their seats. Their dinners rose slowly off the table. Tek craned his neck and slurped up a noodle.

"We gotta get out of this dump," Cale said.

Meanwhile, the cook scuttled along the ceiling and down the wall to the gravity box. "Hold on everybody! I got it! I got it! I got it! Please, please don't panic. Two seconds. Everybody calm, calm." The huge roach-like alien grunted and smashed the gravity box with his bug fist. The gravity box whirred to life and everything in the room that hung suspended in the air immediately crashed to the ground. Cale caught one tray in each hand, and the food plopped unceremoniously—and unappetizingly—back onto them. First the spaghetti, and then the meatballs, which bounced in three different directions, squealing away. Cale winced.

"Ah," he said with a laugh. "Okay. Well, I'm full." He stood and left the commissary, walking down a dark corridor.

"Hey, Cale," said Firrikash with a hiss.

Cale stopped, his stomach sinking. He spotted Po in the shadows. Those two meant nothing but trouble. But when he turned around, he showed no fear.

"Firrikash, Po," he said arrogantly. "How's it going?"

Po glowered at him. "You pulled a nasty stunt back there," he said.

"We don't like your attitude," added Firrikash.

Po nodded. "You've been a little uppity," he said, staring at Cale with his beady stalk eyes.

Cale gulped. "Oh, is that so?" he said coolly. "Whew, well I'm gonna have to work on that." As he spoke, his eyes flickered around the room, looking for a means of escape. There was none. He cracked his knuckles, sizing up the aliens.

The next thing he knew, Firrikash lifted him in a bone-crushing bear hug. One of Po's tentacles slammed into Cale's gut. Cale struggled, but the alien's grip was too strong.

Slam! A chain shot into the room and the two aliens fell to the floor with a loud thud. Cale stared. Who was this man who had just saved him? Firrikash and Po groaned. They couldn't move—their ankles and wrists were bound together. Cale had to give it to the guy—he was fast!

"If you want to hunt humans," said the man, "you should remember that we travel in packs." It was the captain of the *Valkyrie*.

Cale stared at him suspiciously. "What are you doing?" he asked.

"It's commonly known as helping," the captain said sarcastically.

Cale looked away. "Yeah, well, what for?" he asked.

"Sometimes kid," said the man slowly, "people just help each other out."

Cale rolled his eyes. "Oh, right," he said. He gave Po a well-placed kick. "So you're gonna tell me you don't want something in return?" Cale knew the drill. Everybody wanted something out of you. It was the way things worked. Cale walked over to a metal drum filled with water and studied his reflection for a moment. Then he leaned over and splashed water on his face.

Cale had him. "All right, maybe I do," the man admitted.

"What a shock," said Cale.

"I want you to risk your life. I want you to give up everything you have, leave everything you know, and face terror and torture and possibly gruesome death," said the man.

Cale reached down and grabbed a bandanna from around Firrikash's wrist and used it to wipe his face. He blew his nose and tossed the cloth to the floor. He stared at the captain. "And I would want to do that because…"

"Because it's worth it. Because it might do some serious good. Because the human race still matters and you have a chance to prove it. And if that isn't good enough for you, then you're not man enough to handle this mission." The man finished his speech and stared at Cale as if daring him to argue.

"Gosh…" Cale looked down at the floor," I…I never thought of it that way. I guess I've been wrong all these years and it took your inspiring speech to make me see it." Cale's voice began to drip with sarcasm. "You've really changed me. It's beautiful. I…I think we have to hug."

The man looked at Cale with sympathy and put his hand on Cale's shoulder. "Oh man," he said, shaking his head sadly. "They've really ground you down."

The genuine sympathy in the stranger's voice made Cale angry. "Now get this straight!" he sputtered. "I don't even know you! I don't want any part of your mission, and I don't need your help with these oversized morons," he said, gesturing to Firrikash and Po. He kicked them again.

"Oh, okay," the man said, quickly untying the two large aliens. They rose to their feet, glowering at Cale.

"I think he called you morons," said the man.

Cale smiled. The aliens growled and lunged for him. Cale sprinted down the corridor, the aliens hot on his heels.

The captain stared after Cale, deep in thought. When his phone rang, he held up his wrist and hit a button. A light flickered and a tiny glowing human form came into view. "Korso," he said.

"Captain, this is Akima," the young woman said. "We are not alone."

"Are we in good company?" Korso wanted to know.

Akima stared out the window at the three Drej ships. Her brow furrowed. "That's a negative, Captain," she replied. "I think we've fallen in with a very bad crowd."

Korso nodded. "Roger that," he said. "Let's prep for departure. I'll get the package." He shut off his phone, then looked down the hallway where Cale and the aliens had disappeared. "If the package is still in one piece," he said.

● ● ●

Back in the commissary, Cale sidled up to Tek. "Tek, I need to be scarce for a while," he said.

"You don't know the half of it," said Korso, dropping into the seat across from Tek.

Cale stared in disbelief. Him again! "Are you still bothering people?" Cale said. "Hey, go away."

Korso threw back his head and laughed. "Great job with the kid, Tek," he said. "He's a charmer."

Tek smiled. "I expected you to take him off my hands a lot sooner," he replied.

Cale looked from one to the other.

"Tek, who is this guy?" he finally asked. "You know him?"

"Joseph Korso," he said. "I was with your father on the *Titan* project." He reached his hand out to Cale.

Cale looked away. "My father," he said bitterly. "I don't have a father." He turned to Tek. "You brought this guy here?"

"Yes," said Tek.

"I don't understand," said Cale. "Why?"

"You still have that ring your father gave you? Give it to me," Korso commanded.

Cale stared for a moment, confused. Then slowly, he held up his hand. Korso leaned forward and snatched off the ring.

"Hey!" said Cale. "What the heck are you doing?" That was the last thing his father had ever given him and he wanted it back!

With precision, Korso tapped out a series of notches on the inside of the ring with a pen. Beep! The ring began to glow. Korso handed it back to Cale.

"Hmm. Here, put it on," Korso said.

Warily, Cale slipped the ring back on his finger. The ring lit up with glowing circuitry. Cale stared in amazement as what looked like a thin stream of quicksilver ran down his palm and began to unfold into a strangely beautiful filigree tattoo. He blinked. What was happening here?

"It's a storage device," Korso explained. "It's genetically encrypted to your father and, therefore, to you."

Cale was finally able to tear his eyes off his hand. He stared at Korso, hard.

"It's a map, Cale," Korso continued. "Your father's last mission was to hide the *Titan* where the Drej couldn't find it. Well, no one can—except you."

Tek spoke up. "That ship means everything," he said. "Humanity depends upon your finding it."

The enormity of the situation was beginning to dawn on Cale. "Me?" he sputtered. "Whoa, me? No...I'm not…Tek listen," he said, sighing. "There must be someone better."

"It's time, Cale," said Tek softly. "It's time to stop running."

Korso looked up and motioned toward the doorway. "Well, actually," he said, "I think it's time to start."

CHAPTER 3

Cale looked toward the door. Three Drej guards stood there, guns at the ready. Their blue metallic bodies glowed ominously.

"Drej?" said Cale. "What do they want?"

"They want you, kid," Korso replied. "Same way I want you, only dead."

This was ridiculous! Why would the Drej be interested in him! "How do you know they want me dead?" Cale asked. Suddenly, the Drej spotted him and leveled their weapons—right at his head.

"Whoa! I'm convinced!" said Cale. Korso reached out his arm and knocked Cale to the ground. The Drej opened fire, lasers beaming just inches above Cale's head. Korso kicked a nearby table to the ground, using it for cover as he returned fire. He hit one of the Drej, who fell to the floor.

"We've got to get to the kitchen!" Korso yelled. Cale looked—the doorway was all the way across the commis-

sary, and there wasn't much cover. Cale searched frantically for another option.

"Korso!" he shouted. "The gravity drive!"

Korso spun around, nailing the box with a blast from his
gun. Everything started floating. Korso fired again at the
Drej, and the force of the blast sent them careening against
the wall. This bought them the time they needed.

"You ready?" said Korso.

Cale turned to his friend. "Tek, I'll lead you in," he said.

"I'll stay here," said Tek gently.

"Tek, you can't!" yelled Cale.

"Take care of the kid," Tek told his old friend, Korso.
"He's not all grown up yet."

"No, no, no, no," Cale protested. "You're coming."

Tek smiled. "Go Cale," he said softly. "I'll read about
you."

Korso braced himself and fired a couple of shots to the
doorway, then leapt into midair. "Follow me!" he shouted.

He fired a blast at a wall and the force rocketed him
backward over the serving counter and into the kitchen.
Crash! Pots and pans went flying. Cale was still behind the
table when the Drej hit it with a powerful blast, which sent
him, too, into the kitchen. A metal pot sat rakishly on his

head. "Well, this would be good if we had any baking to do!" he said.

Hiss! What was that noise? Korso spun toward the door. The Drej were cutting through the door with a laser torch! The cook, perched on the ceiling, was very angry. "Oh, my food!" he yelled. "You guys are terrible! You…you're unsanitary! Oh, I hope that they catch you and I'll testify against you, and you'll never get out of jail!"

Just then, laser fire raked the room. "Drej!" said the cook, his anger forgotten. "Ooh…I've gotta go now!" He scuttled through an open vent in the ceiling and disappeared. Korso stared after him. "Follow ugly," he said, jerking his thumb toward the vent. Cale launched himself upwards, Korso right behind him.

"Oh great," Cale said with a sigh. "Yeah, no one would ever think of looking for us in the vent."

"Go!" thundered Korso.

Meanwhile, the Drej had finished cutting out the lock and kicked in the door. They fired into the room and then realized the kitchen was empty. Their gazes fell on the open vent. They would find the boy yet.

• • •

"Go! Go! Go!" yelled Korso. They rushed past the cook.

The cook was running as fast as his many insect legs would carry him and pushed past them. "Oh, come on," he said, panting. "Why is this happening to me?"

The vent led to a room with a round pipe in the middle. Cale and Korso quickly climbed down it, not knowing where it would lead. The cook panicked, racing around the room like a frightened insect. The Drej caught up and found him, his antennae waving wildly in fear. "Hi," said the cook. "They went right down there. They came into my kitchen and they ruined the place…"

Irritated, the Drej blasted the cook. His guts exploded in a flash of bright green alien blood.

• • •

Where were they? Cale crawled out of the pipe and looked around. They were in the ship's repair hangar, surrounded by vessels in various states of repair.

"We've gotta get out of here!" Korso exclaimed. He gestured to a sleek fightercraft parked in front of them. "Go!" he said.

They made a run for it, just as the two Drej dropped into the room, blasting away at them. Korso knocked over a fuel canister and kicked it at the Drej. He aimed, fired—and the canister exploded into flames. It gave them just the time they needed.

Cale immediately climbed into the driver's seat, but Korso pushed him aside. "Maybe next time kid," he said.

"Hey, I can fly it too!" Cale protested.

Korso began deftly flicking on all the switches, lighting up the ship's controls. Cale, all the while, was keeping his eyes peeled for the Drej. Things were happening so fast. Where was he going? What was he going to do without Tek?

Korso let out his breath. "It won't start!"

"I've got an idea," said Cale. He leapt out of the craft and stood on the back, working with some wires. Suddenly, the thrusters fired to life and the ship instantly took off. Cale grabbed onto the ship, barely hanging on. A few Drej ships arrived and took aim at Cale. One of the shots winged him and he lost his grip, plummeting down. He fell hard onto the wing of a docked ship.

Korso expertly maneuvered the fightercraft back around.

"Hang on kid, I'm comin'!" he shouted. As Korso neared, Cale made a death-defying leap onto the moving ship. Just as he landed on the glass roof, Korso accelerated hard toward the main doors of the hangar. But they were closing. The Drej were cutting off their only means of escape!

"They're locking down the doors!" Cale shouted.

"Not going forward," said Korso. "Going up."

"Up?" said Cale. He looked up—and saw a huge sky-light of paneled glass. Korso couldn't be serious, could he? Cale jumped inside the ship and gulped as it began to rise. Korso was serious.

CRASH! The ship smashed through the glass dome. Everyone on the concourse began to panic. They scattered as the ship hovered overhead, looking for a way out. Korso slammed on the thrusters. The ship lurched forward down the concourse, running the length of the docking bay arm. The sheer force slammed Cale back in his seat. Then he looked ahead—his stomach sank as he saw the heavy vac-uum shields begin to rise out of the floor and down from the ceiling of each bay mouth. Within seconds, the two doors would meet, closing off the bays and destroying their only chance for escape.

"You should brace yourself," Korso warned.

"Ah, yeah, I was feeling that," said Cale. He looked from Korso to the rapidly closing bay doors and back to Korso again. Was this guy for real? The doors were nearly closed. There was no way they would fit. But Korso still kept speeding towards them. Cale stared. This man was insane!

"Eject," Korso said. He stared at the controls. "Where's the eject?" he said, his voice rising. Cale could definitely hear a note of panic creeping into Korso's voice. "Cale, this model does have an eject, right?"

Cale leaned forward and hit the eject button. The two were slammed back in their seats as the escape pod of the ship fired out from the rest of the hull. The pod crashed through the glass ceiling of the docking arm. A split second later, the abandoned body of the ship smashed into the vacuum shields. Cale watched, his mouth open, as it exploded into a massive fireball.

Korso was his cocky self again. "And you were worried," he said with a laugh.

The pod tumbled around and around until Korso stabilized it. Just then, Cale noticed a spider web of pressure cracks spreading across the windshield. Korso noticed them too. He couldn't hide his shocked expression.

"What do you mean *were*?" said Cale.

Korso picked up the radio. "Akima, we need a pick up here," he said.

"It's a little late for that," said Cale.

Inside the cockpit of the *Valkyrie*, Akima maneuvered the ship, peering through the windshield to find her captain and his friend. Finally, she spotted them on the radar screen.

"I'm right above you. Can you get to me?" she said.

"Not enough time..." Cale managed to say. The pressure cracks were spreading and they were running out of air. "Not...not...not a lot of time."

Thinking quickly, Korso kicked open a panel by his feet. A fire extinguisher floated out into the weightless cabin. Well, this would have to do! He grabbed for it, then grabbed Cale by the collar.

"Exhale," he told him.

Cale stared at him. This guy was truly crazy! "You've got to be kidding!"

"Exhale..." said Korso in a warning tone.

"Oh no, no!" yelled Cale. When he realized Korso was indeed serious, he had no choice but to comply. As he exhaled all the air out of his lungs, Korso did the same. Then he forcefully kicked the windshield. It exploded outward in a shower of glass and the two flew out of the cabin and into space. Korso used the pressure from the extinguisher as an altitude jet, steering them toward the belly of the *Valkyrie*, which waited patiently overhead. They flew inside and the bay doors slid neatly shut.

The two lay there, unconscious for a moment or two. Finally, Korso woke up.

"Cale, Cale, you alive?" he asked.

Cale's eyes fluttered open. "Uh, maybe," he said. "Hey, my skin feels weird."

"That's because your blood froze," explained Korso.

It took a moment for Cale to process that. "Oh. That explains it," he said.

His head fell back and he blacked out again.

• • •

When Cale next awoke, he was very confused. Where was he? And who was looking down at him so tenderly? He blinked as Akima's face swam into focus. He smiled as he recognized her. He couldn't explain the feeling that he had, but he knew that he felt safe and secure with Akima near. The next thing he knew, a funny-looking face poked into view. "Is it dead?" it asked. "Can we eat him?"

Cale panicked. "No! It's not dead! Who are you? Go away!" Cale began to struggle. That's when he noticed that he was being held in place by a wide beam of light. Even worse, he was naked.

"Hey! What's going on! Why am I naked?" he shouted.

"Preed," Akima said to the hungry alien. "You're in my light."

"Ah, such motherly concern for the subject!" Preed teased. He held a tray full of instruments. "Why, you positively glow with maternal warmth, Akima. It's very fetching."

"I'm still naked here," Cale reminded them.

Akima smiled down at the patient. "Relax," she said. "We're just making sure you didn't get all broken." She turned to Preed. "Hand me the probe."

Uh-oh. Cale didn't like the sound of that! "The probe?" he said in a panicked voice. "Where does the probe go?"

Akima brandished a large, glowing, oddly-shaped thermometer-like thing in her hand.

"You know, I'm really feeling much better!" said Cale. "Ow!" he yelled as Akima stabbed him in the hip with the probe.

"This is just great," complained Akima. "Cross half the galaxy, nearly get our butts shot off by the Drej, just so we can rescue the window washer."

Cale was insulted. "Hey, for your information," he said with as much dignity as he could muster, considering he was still quite naked, "I happen to be humanity's last great hope."

Preed shook his head sadly. "I weep for the species."

"You're fine," said Akima, hitting a lever with her foot. The beam of light moved Cale into a standing position.

"Yeah, I'm the guy with the map here," Cale bragged, trying to impress Akima. "This is big medicine, right?"

"Big medicine, let me see," said Akima.

Cale held out his hand indifferently. But the way Akima gently took it into her own and stared at it so reverently… "This is really it," she breathed. "This can save us…"

Cale was speechless. "Yeah, I guess," he said. Akima gently ran her finger along his palm.

"Do you know what this means?" she asked.

Cale laughed uncomfortably. "I'm really wanting those pants right about now."

Preed appeared. "Akima, my pet, if the boy isn't at death's door, Korso wants Gune to check the map so we can set a course. Do you mind? Are we through pawing? This is the *Valkyrie,* not a singles bar!"

Akima and Cale both blushed and looked away. "We're done," she said in a clipped tone.

Cale was mortified and decided to change the subject. "You know," he said, "I never said I was going to help you guys. We never addressed what's in it for me."

"Why, you get to be a hero," said Preed with a shrug, tossing Cale his boots.

"A hero?" said Cale with disbelief. Was that all? "Come on. I mean, there must be something on the *Titan* worth selling or trading...or...What, we're gonna risk our necks to help a bunch of Drifter Colony bums?" He stopped talking. "Where are my pants?"

The next thing he knew, his pants hit him square in the face. He pulled them away in time to see Akima stalk out of the room angrily.

"Guess where Akima grew up?" said Preed in a mocking tone.

Cale grimaced. Big mistake. "Uh, Drifter Colony?"

Preed nodded. "Yes, the boy learns," he said.

CHAPTER 4

"**L**ook, where's Korso?" Cale asked, anxiously waiting for some answers. He was finally dressed and he and Preed were walking down the *Valkyrie's* corridor.

"I believe he's in navigation," replied Preed. "We're headed there now."

A huge alien, who looked sort of like a kangaroo, lumbered toward them carrying a large steel toolbox. Muttering under her breath in her native tongue, she ran right into Cale, knocking him to the ground.

"You want to watch who you're stepping on?" said Cale angrily.

The alien looked down at Cale—in her eyes, just another puny human. "Or you'll *what*?" she snarled.

Preed stepped in. "Ah, the lovely and talented Stith," he said. "This is Cale. You remember Cale?"

Stith growled and continued down the hallway. "No, no, no," she muttered. "Cannot talk. We lost targeting on one of our aft gun turrets again. What do you think this ship is, a ferry ride?" Just then her toolbox suddenly spilled open and the contents tumbled to the floor in an angry crash. She groaned. Loudly.

Preed turned to Cale. "She's a sweet little thing," he explained. "Weapons specialist. Normally, she's very good natured."

Was this guy fooling with him? Cale looked back at the still-muttering Stith. Good natured? Her?

"Great! Things aren't bad enough!" Stith moaned. "Darn tools all over the floor!"

Stith reached back with one massive foot and kicked the toolbox with all of her might. It slammed into the wall, a huge dent in its side.

When they reached a steel door marked "Navigation," Preed knocked.

They could hear a voice inside. "Okay, must go to Plan B. Yes, must go to Plan B," it muttered.

"Gune!" Preed called. "Guney! Are you in there?"

Crash! Gune continued to mumble. "Okay, I must multiply the mass by the acceleration, multiply the coefficient of the friction, apply the necessary force…"

Preed opened the door a crack. "Gune?" he said. No answer. Cale and Preed stepped inside the navigation room. Inventions were everywhere. A dimensional map of the stars and planets caught Cale's eyes and he stepped forward to take a better look. "Whoa. Look at that," he said.

"Does this look familiar?" said Gune, a brilliant, muttering alien with huge eyes. Cale stared. It wasn't that Gune sort of looked like a cross between a huge turtle and a monstrous frog. Cale certainly had seen his share of strange-looking aliens in his lifetime. It was just that Gune seemed, well, a little off. Gune held his hand out to Preed. In it was a small spherical object. "Do you know what it is? Neither do I!"

Gune turned away, shrugging. "I made it last night in my sleep. Apparently, I used gindrogac. Highly unstable."

"Gune?" said Preed.

"I put a button on it," Gune continued. "Yes, I wish to press it, but I'm not sure what will happen if I do."

Preed looked irritated. Cale, meanwhile, was studying the star map. The device was turning, but was slightly out of whack. Cale began hitting some keys. "Hmmm. Let me see now…3, 5, 22, 74,…11."

Gune was worried. "Ah, no!" he said. "No, no, no, no. Careful. Please, please."

He stared, his breath held. But the device began to spin smoothly. Whatever Cale did, it worked.

"It's perfect!" Cale said. He was quite pleased with himself.

"Oh, yes!" said Gune. "Perfect!"

Cale laughed. "So where are we now?" he wanted to know.

"We are here, right here," Gune said, pointing. "The Bellasan Quadrant."

"About three million keks from Tau-14," Preed explained. "Why, are you homesick?"

Cale rolled his eyes. "Gotta have a home for that," he said.

Gune was suddenly intrigued by his human visitor. He began poking at him. "Hmmm," he mused. "Translucent bi-pedal mesomorphic embryonic male!" he said.

"Yes, yes, yes, this is all very fascinating," said Preed impatiently. He grabbed Cale's hand and held it up to Gune. "But take a look at this. It's a map. Can you read it?"

"Can I read it?" said Gune indignantly. "Of course I can read it. Yes! Hmmm."

Gune grabbed Cale's hand, yanking it toward him as if he were surprised it was attached to Cale's arm. Cale almost fell over. That hurt!

"So what do you see?" Cale asked.

Gune studied his hand intently. "Yes," he said. "This is Pl'ochda. And this...this...this is Solbrecht. And this, and this, and this, what is this?" he asked, puzzled.

Cale looked down. "That's uh...lunch," he said.

"Oh, it's lunch!" said Gune happily. He licked Cale's hand. "Mmm. Spaghetti derivative. Meatballs, sort of anyway, and Caldrach droppings. Who ate it before you did?" he said, slurping away.

"Hey, hey," said Cale, wrenching his arm away and backing off. Of all the creatures he had met on the *Valkyrie* so far, Gune may have been the most unusual, but Cale was starting to feel a special bond with him.

Gune giggled wildly.

Cale turned to Preed. "I'll tell you a secret," Cale said under his breath. "This guy's nuts."

"I'll tell you another," said a voice. Cale spun around. It was Korso. "He's never wrong. Where are we going, Gune?"

Gune proudly showed the captain his map. "The broken moon of Sesharrim," he said. "Only thirteen thousand keks away."

Korso turned to Preed. "Have Akima lay a course," he commanded. Preed left for the bridge, pausing for a moment to whisper in Korso's ear.

Cale tried to make sense of everything he had heard so far. "And that's where the *Titan* is?" he asked.

"No, no, no," said Gune impatiently. "This is broken moon. This is mystery for thinking about. Yes, not clear… not clear."

Korso shrugged. "Well, it's a start," he said. "Come on kid, I'll buy you a drink."

Back in Korso's quarters, Cale and the captain stared as the jerry-rigged vending machine dispensed one drop of thick green goop.

"She's a little bit twitchy," explained Korso. "Hold on." He drew back and gave the machine a vicious kick. The spigot and several nuts and bolts dropped into the cup. Without being asked, Cale turned his attention to the machine. He just couldn't help himself. He loved machines and instinctively knew how they worked. He fiddled and rigged away as he spoke.

"So what's on this broken moon place, anyway?" Cale asked.

"The Gaoul," said Korso. "They're the only intelligent race on the planet. Least, that's what I've heard."

Cale studied a wire. "And they'll lead us to the *Titan*?" he asked.

Korso smirked. "That wouldn't be interest in your voice, would it?"

Cale looked up from the machine. "Hey, the *Titan's* my ticket. Anything people are willing to kill me for has got to be worth some meaningful cash."

"Oh, I get it!" said Korso, nodding. "We're playing tough guy!"

Cale walked up to Korso and got right in his face. "Look in my eyes," he said. "You see me playing?"

Korso stared back. "I see your father."

Cale stepped back. A wave of emotions came over him—hurt, anger, and even pride. He looked down—he was very confused. There was a moment of silence. Just then, the vending machine whirred to life. A perfect cup of aromatic green brew was poured.

Korso looked at Cale levelly. "He was good with machines, too."

Cale shifted uncomfortably. "Yeah, well, I don't remember," he said with a shrug.

"He built the *Titan*," explained Korso as he sat down. "Most advanced ship in the universe. Fully self-sustaining energy system—the science was way beyond the rest of us—but he believed it was the key to finding a new homeworld. He said in time…"

"In time?!?" Cale exploded. "How much time? If he knew about another world for the human race, why not just tell us where it is?"

"This wasn't Plan A kid," said Korso. "Your father knew the Drej would come after him. That's why he left the map with you."

Watching the stars speed by was a beautiful sight that had an almost hypnotic effect on Cale. It calmed him a little.

"Before he died, your father hid the *Titan*. The only way to find it is in your hand."

Cale turned to him. "So you're really counting on me then," he said.

"We all are," Korso explained.

Cale narrowed his eyes. "Well, if I don't like the way things are going, I'll show you how much like my father I really am."

Korso looked at him curiously.

Cale took a swig of his green liquid. "I'll leave," he said.

CHAPTER 5

The broken moon loomed before the *Valkyrie*. Cale stared at the huge cleft down the middle. He could only imagine what ancient force had caused such massive destruction. As the ship moved forward, the water planet Sesharrim suddenly came into view. Light rippled across its red ocean. The surface was studded with bright red shapes. Cale didn't know it, but those were long-dead coral clusters, which had risen above sea level eons ago. Akima steered the ship down and Cale almost gasped at the sight. An arched reef sheltered the ruins of an ancient and magnificent city. The spires and towers virtually covered the exposed surface of the coral. Massive hydrogen trees stood like guards along the shoreline. They floated high in the air, tethered to the water by their thin twisted roots.

"No place to set down on the island," said Korso. Just then, he spied a small, flat formation of coral in the water a few miles from the larger formation. "Land on that coral reef," he commanded.

The *Valkyrie* spiraled down towards the landing site, coming to rest on the plateau.

• • •

Korso, Akima, Cale, and Stith stood in the hoversled as it sat in the water just below the *Valkyrie*. Preed and Gune watched from the shore.

"We'll take the sled," Korso said, "and see if we can locate the Gaoul. Preed, you and Gune watch the ship."

Gune was disappointed. He always had to stay behind. "Watch the ship?" he asked.

Korso ignored him. "And keep the engines hot," he finished.

Preed nodded. "Oh, yes. They'll be nice and toasty. I'm not keen on the Drej catching me with my trousers down."

Everyone piled on and the hoversled roared away, Akima at the controls. They approached the main island. Korso put a fatherly arm around Cale's shoulder as the two scanned the horizon. "Welcome to planet Sesharrim, Cale," he said. Cale sniffed the air, wrinkling his nose. Phew! "It stinks!" he said.

"Hydrogen trees," Korso explained. "Clip one of those and we'll be blown to steaming bits."

Cale cringed slightly as Akima winded the ship through the dangling roots. But there was no need to be wary—Akima was an expert pilot.

They reached the ruins of the city. It had an eerie majesty to it, with its broken columns and the Greek temple-like structures that cast long, dark shadows. In the center square of the city, the foursome stopped and looked around.

"Hello!" yelled Korso. "Anybody there? We're looking for the Gaoul."

"What exactly do the Gaoul look like?" Cale asked Akima.

Akima didn't know. Neither did Stith. "Don't know," said Korso. "They don't get out much."

Cale stopped. Was that a flash of light he just saw over Korso's shoulder? He turned around. Stith saw it too. Another light flashed atop a distant column. Then it winked out.

"We have a kid with a map here that you guys should know about," Korso called out.

Cale was just about to argue at Korso's use of "kid"—he was twenty years old for goodness' sake—when he was distracted by a rushing noise rising from the distance. Korso held his rifle at the ready, gesturing for Cale to take a pistol from his belt.

Cale blinked. What was happening? A red cloud emerged from underneath the arch of the island. He squinted and could hardly believe what he saw—there were hundreds of flying creatures heading toward them. He stared in amazement. They were tall, thin, crimson-red creatures with leathery, bat-like wings, sharp triangular heads, and glowing white eyes. In a word—they were frightening. The sound of a thousand flapping wings was unlike anything Cale had ever heard before.

The creatures circled the group, then began to descend, landing on every available perch, surrounding them and cutting off any means of escape. Suddenly, they screamed, wild terrifying cries. The group huddled, backs together, their guns at the ready. Cale was absolutely terrified.

"I think we know what happened to the Gaoul," said Korso warily. Everyone nodded. These horrible creatures must have wiped out every last one of them! "Stith!" Korso said. "Give me an option here!"

"Blast 'em?" suggested Stith. That was always her first reaction.

"That's creative," Korso said.

"I'm in!" said Cale. And he meant it.

The creatures moved closer, staring at them intently, their glowing white eyes blinking eerily. Akima noticed that they seemed to be looking only at Cale.

"Open fire on five," said Korso. "We'll clear a path to the sled. Everybody ready? One... two..."

Cale gulped and, along with the rest of the group, took aim as more creatures landed. They signaled to each other with synchronized flaps of their wings.

"Wait! No stop!" said Akima. "Stop! Look what they're doing!"

Korso brushed her off. "If these things killed the Gaoul, what makes you think that..."

"Wait!" said Akima. "I think they *are* the Gaoul!"

• • •

Chirp! Preed found the noisy little cricket in his gun sights and fired at the tiny creature. He shot again and again as the cricket hopped around, merrily eluding the singing bullets. Preed got more and more impatient. Finally, he stopped shooting and started stomping the ground madly with his boots. Crunch! He was pretty sure he got him! Preed had a satisfied look on his face, but only for a moment.

Chirp! The cricket started singing again. Preed growled in frustration. "Quick little devil!" he said with a laugh.

Inside the *Valkyrie* bridge, Gune spun around in his chair as he played with his latest invention—a floating pyramid. He mumbled away to himself, not noticing the warning red light flashing and the beeping coming from the console.

"Okay, all I have to do is tap into the central computer and re-configure the departure protocols. Yes…making progress, yes, I'm making progress!" He laughed out loud. "Wait, wait, hmmm!"

• • •

By this time, the Gaoul had completely circled the group, pale light spilling from their many glowing eyes. Cale held his hand up to them, letting them check the markings. The creatures' wings rustled as they moved closer to get a better look. They parted to let an older creature through. He slowly walked through the crowd, his back bent and twisted. It was the Gaoul chief and medicine man. He studied Cale intently. Then, with a sweeping motion, the chief lifted one leathery wing to the sky. Cale watched, not understanding. The chief did it again. Cale looked up to the heavens.

"The moon," said Cale. "Yeah. That's how we knew to come here." He held out his hand to the chief. "My father made a map with that moon on it. Why? Is the ship hidden there?"

The chief grabbed Cale by his shoulders and turned him to face the moon. Then it reached out its wing again. Cale didn't understand. Only when the chief repeated the action two more times, did Cale understand that he was meant to do the same. Cale slowly raised his hand to eclipse the stars…and gasped as four stars in the sky lined up with the space between each finger. It was a perfect fit.

Korso and Akima looked up. The map on Cale's hand clearly pointed to a distant cluster of stars.

"It's somewhere in the Andali Nebula," said Akima.

"I'll be darned," said Korso, shaking his head. "We did it, kid," he said to Cale. "The *Titan* is as good as ours."

But Cale, lost in his thoughts, barely heard him. "He must have been here," he said softly. "Standing here. Right here." He shook his head, unbelievingly. To stand in the same place his father had once stood, to be on the very mission his father had died trying to complete, was almost too much for him to take.

"Who?" asked Akima.

"My father," replied Cale.

Suddenly, the sky grew dark. Everyone looked up. The heavens were filled with many midnight blue Drej ships. The ships spotted them and began swooping down.

"Go!" shouted Korso.

Stith, Akima, Cale, and Korso sprinted through the ruins of Sesharrim toward the hoversled, the Drej close behind. As the stinger ships bore down on the city, the huge mass of Gaoul rose up in flight.

"We've got to get to the beach!" Korso shouted. Cale started running as fast as he could. Suddenly, the flapping of wings was very loud—and he felt himself being lifted into the air. He looked around frantically, then realized that the Gaoul were helping him and the rest of his party to safety.

The Gaoul flapped their wings as fast as they could, the Drej in hot pursuit, firing away.

"Why aren't they shooting at Cale?" Akima yelled.

"They must want him alive!" Korso shouted back.

A ship came after Cale, and the Gaoul who was carrying him lost his grip. Cale gulped as he plummeted toward the water. But then another Gaoul caught him in mid-air, upside down.

"Nice catch!" said Cale appreciatively. The creature flew off, narrowly missing the bulbous hydrogen trees. Another Drej ship began its attack and once again, Cale began to fall. This time, he hit the water with a loud splash. He swam underwater, then realized that another Drej stinger was still on his tail! He tried to swim away, but he was not fast enough. The ship lifted him out of the water and into the air. Luckily, a watchful Gaoul plucked him off the ship's roof and took him to the hoversled.

Once everyone was safe on the hoversled, the Gaoul took off. The sled roared to life. Stith opened fire with the hand cannon. She took out two Drej ships, which sent a third crashing into another. Four down—too many to go.

Korso desperately tried to radio the *Valkyrie*. "Preed, come in! Preed, where are you?" But there was no answer.

Akima turned to Cale. "Hold on!" she said, pointing to a cable loop. They were in for a bumpy ride!

• • •

Meanwhile, back at the *Valkyrie*, Gune finally noticed that the radar screen was flashing wildly behind him. He gasped and raced for the door. He was panting and his eyes were wild. "Preed, Preed, Preed!" Gune shouted. "Aren't you supposed to be watching out for the Drej?"

Preed turned around wearily. "Yes, caveman that's right. Drej bad, we good. Now go look at something shiny for a while." He turned back to the gun. "How's this?" he asked, blasting away at the cricket once more.

"Oh! Ooh! Well, you'd better look again!" Gune said.

Preed looked up and saw a sky full of stars, nothing more. He was just about to make a sarcastic comment when he looked once more and saw...

"Drej!" they both shouted.

• • •

The hoversled raced across the Sesharrim Ocean, followed by the Gaoul. The Drej fired away, hitting some of the winged creatures. They plummeted into the sea. Cale carefully watched the ships. One broke formation and circled to the side, out of Stith's line of sight. There was only one thing to do. Letting go of the cable loop, Cale readied, aimed, and fired. His shot found its mark, hitting the stinger ship in the port engine. The ship was sent spinning in a fireball. But Cale paid the price for his daring, as he too, was sent reeling.

Preed radioed Korso. "Captain, we're on our way. We can't see you. Where are you?"

"We're in the hydrogen trees being charged by the Drej," Korso replied. "See if you can spot them—quick!" He turned to his pilot. "Akima…"

"Hang on!" she shouted, thrusting the ship backwards to avoid the stingers.

"Nice move!" Korso yelled.

"Come on," said Preed. "Show yourselves!"

Just then, Cale lost his balance. "Whoa!" he shouted as he fell off the sled.

"Cale!" yelled Akima in a panicked voice. She dove after him, grabbing his ankle. But she too found herself being dragged off the sled. They both fell into the sea. Neither Stith nor Korso noticed that the two were missing. Akima surfaced first. She was out of breath, but she wasn't hurt. Cale popped up next. Akima glared at him.

"I got them!" Cale said proudly.

"Terrific!" said Akima sarcastically.

Cale pushed her underwater as laserbolts from the Drej ship sizzled past them.

Stith continued to fire at the approaching Drej ships. Click click click click. She was out of ammo. Korso turned around to see what was going on. For the first time, he noticed that Cale and Akima were missing. "Darn it!" he said. But there was no turning back. The Drej were too close. It would be a death wish.

• • •

In the ocean, Cale and Akima treaded water, trying to stay afloat. They looked up in time to see a Drej stinger racing close. Cale fired off four shots with his pistol. Two hit, and the ship veered off. But Cale and Akima's feelings of victory were momentary as a second ship swooped down, a hot green beam shooting out of its belly. Before they realized what was happening, they were lifted right out of the ocean. Cale and Akima tumbled around in the energy field as the ship lifted them up. Cale tried to fire, but his pistol would not shoot.

As the remaining stinger ships fell into a V-formation, Cale and Akima were carried into one of the ships. They all took off.

From the smoking hoversled, Korso watched the Drej ships take off. The *Valkyrie* swooped overhead, blowing three stingers out of the sky with a bright flash.

"Don't shoot! Don't shoot!" shouted Korso into his walkie-talkie to Preed. "They've got Cale!"

The swarm of Drej ships headed back toward the mothership.

The *Valkyrie* hovered over the water and Stith and Korso boarded the ship. Stith muttered to herself, angry that she had not protected Cale. But she was ready to point the finger elsewhere.

Korso began issuing orders. "Gune, calculate their trajectory. Stith, take weapons. Let's get it on, people!"

Stith glared at Preed. "Nice job covering our butts!" she said.

"Well, you're the weapons expert!" retorted Preed.

Stith blew her top. "What were you doing, taking a nap?" she thundered.

Korso had had enough. "Okay, we lost our meal ticket," he said. "But they are not going to get away with it." He pointed his finger angrily into the air for emphasis.

"Well, let's quit running our collective mouths and go get him!" Stith said.

Korso nodded solemnly. "Our only chance to rescue them is to track Akima. Stith, get on it."

CHAPTER 6

The Drej stinger ship holding Cale and Akima raced through space, headed toward the mothership with its precious cargo. The two were being held prisoner in a holding cell. Akima looked out a porthole, seeing nothing but vast, empty space. She shook her head. "They're gonna use you to figure out where the *Titan* is. Probably just blow it up too, when they find it."

"We have to find a way out of here, or we're dead," Cale said.

Akima sighed. "No question about that," she replied. "Maybe Korso will get to the *Titan* first."

Cale studied Akima. "Why do you care so much about that thing?"

"I was raised around people," Akima explained, turning to face him. "Drifter Colony bums, I believe is the term."

Cale looked at his feet, still embarrassed.

"I barely remember Earth," Akima continued, "but the older ones used to tell us about it so it would never be completely lost. No matter how hard things got—and they were hard—those memories kept us going. Once we had a home. The *Titan* is our chance to find one again." She stared ahead, lost in reverie. Cale put his hand on her shoulder. "I guess that's how I ended up here," she finished softly. Akima sat down, and Cale joined her. The two sat in silence. Cale couldn't remember feeling so close to another person in a long, long time.

"Why don't they just kill all of us?" Cale wondered aloud. "Why don't the Drej just wipe out the human race?"

Akima shrugged. "Waste of energy. Without a planet, we're no longer a threat."

"Well, they must have changed their minds," said Cale softly. There was a loud swoosh and the two looked at each other. The small stinger was now inside the Drej mothership. What was in store for them, neither of them knew. But they realized that it could not be good.

• • •

The ship disappeared, leaving Cale and Akima in the middle of a huge structure surrounded by Drej. They blinked, unaccustomed to the powerful lights that pulsated all around them. It was eerie and strangely disorienting. When Akima's eyes adjusted, she could finally take in the magnitude of the mothership. She could hardly believe what she was seeing. With a sharp intake of breath, she looked down and saw that Cale was kneeling on the ground. "Cale, are you okay?" she asked. Just then, she was yanked away from him by an unseen, powerful force and was pinned to a nearby wall.

"Akima!" shouted Cale. He tried to run toward her, but was immediately blasted into the air by a beam of light. Bolts of lightning shot from his arms and legs and the map on his hand began to glow eerily.

"No!" he screamed. There was a flash of light. The Drej were locking in on the coordinates of Cale's map. "Nooooo!" yelled Cale. His father's life's work…all for nothing. But it was too late. Now the Drej knew where the *Titan* was located—the Andali Nebula. Once the Drej had the information they needed, Cale plummeted back to the floor.

• • •

Suddenly, in an enormous sphere hanging above him, the dark and evil face of the Drej queen appeared before Cale. He could not believe his ears. The voice was neither

Humanity flees the Drej onslaught.

The Drej mothership hovers over Earth. Queen Drej, ruler of her alien race, orders: "Now we finish it . . ."

Cale becomes a refugee on Tau-14,
a third-rate asteroid.

As Cale's ring begins to glow, a map
appears upon his palm.

The indestructible Drej hunt for Cale.

The *Valkyrie* soars in over the forest of hydrogen trees.

The broken moon of Sesharrim holds the key to the *Titan's* location.

Chief Gaoul points Cale to the Andali Nebula.

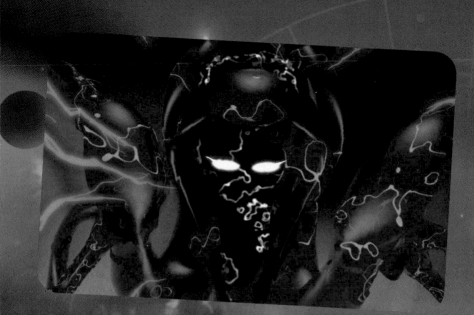

The evil Drej queen vows to destroy the *Titan*.

Cale uses his hand to part the energy forcefield.

Korso shouts at the Drej queen, "We had a deal!"

Cale and Akima set off in the newly repaired
Phoenix in search of the *Titan*.

Carefully maneuvering through the Ice Rings of Tigrin.

"The Drej said they'd let me live—
provided I kill all of you."

Channeling the pure energy of the Drej to start the *Titan*.

"I think I'll call it . . . Bob!"

male nor female. Neither human nor alien. He wanted to cover his ears to block out the sound.

"We have our destination. Set a course for the nebula. Keep the boy on board, he may yet be useful. Discard the girl."

Cale rose to his feet and ran forward. "No! Stop! Leave her alone!" he howled.

Akima was immediately flung into the air and sealed in a glass coffin-like structure. She was then sucked out the wall of the Drej ship and flung into space.

"Akimaaaaaaa!" Cale screamed. But there was nothing he could do. Akima was gone.

• • •

The next thing he knew, he was sucked through the floor and dropped into a prison cell. Its strange walls pulsed with electricity. Cale pounded the floor and screamed in frustration. Finally, he calmed himself down and stared at the glowing walls. He reached out to touch it with his finger—and got the nastiest shock of his life. Cale fell to the ground.

• • •

The bazaar was crowded with buyers and sellers. But this was no ordinary selling place—the commodity here was humans.

Preed yelled at his human "slave." "Come along you worthless speck of human pocket lint. Mush!"

His stooped-over human "slave" turned around and glowered at him. "I think you're enjoying this!" Korso said.

"Shhh!" warned Stith. "They're just up ahead."

Soon they reached an alien guard. Stith turned to Preed, ready for action. "All right," she said. "I'll take out the guard."

"Easy big girl!" Preed said in a warning voice. "This requires cunning and deception." And he knew he was just the alien for the job. He grabbed Korso and dragged him up the steps to where the guard waited.

"Hello," Preed said pleasantly to the guard.

"Ugh," the horned alien guard grunted back.

"Uh, I'm an Akrennian trader," Preed said, not so smoothly. "I wonder if we might sneak a peek at the new shipment of human slaves before they go on the market."

"You're not allowed," said the guard with finality.

"Traditionally, no," said Preed. "You're absolutely right. But you see I need a new slave rather badly," he explained, slapping Korso on the back of the head. "Stop fidgeting worm!" he yelled. He turned back to the guard. "And I can't wait till auction. I have to be on the shuttle. I have an appointment to have my ear shaved. It has to be booked months in advance. You see my problem."

The guard whipped out a gun and leveled it at the three. "You're lying," he said. "He's not a slave, and you're not traders."

Preed was flabbergasted. He thought he had done a fine job! "But…I…how?"

The guard jerked his head toward Korso. "Look at the way he stands. He doesn't carry himself like a slave. Probably ex-military." He then pointed to Preed. "Akrennian traders always threaten before they ask a favor. It's tradition." He indicated Stith. "And your robes are made out of bedspreads."

Preed turned toward the others. "Just out of curiosity, did we have a Plan B?" he asked.

Stith kicked the guard with one of her massive legs, knocking him against the door. Korso ran forward and opened the door as Preed and Stith stepped over the guard's motionless body. He was out cold.

"Hmmm," mused Preed. "An intelligent guard. Didn't see that one coming."

Meanwhile, Cale was still figuring out a way to escape. He rocked back and forth in anger and frustration. The Drej had stolen his father's secret. And worst of all—Akima was gone, probably dead. Cale stared, unseeing, at the prison cell wall. Suddenly, he focused on the patterns of energy pulsing across it. His eyes narrowed—he had an idea. Cale stood and leaned close to the pulsing wall, studying it intently. Then he reached out his finger again, prepared for the shock. Fighting the searing pain, he placed his other hand on the wall and slowly brought his two hands together. The energy swirled around it, flashing as his hands partially penetrated the solid surface of the wall. Cale gritted his teeth and smiled—he was almost there. There was another flash across the wall's surface and Cale pushed his way free! Everything except for his foot! He could hear the marching feet of approaching Drej soldiers. He pulled and pulled and finally wrenched his trapped foot free, just in time to dive for cover.

• • •

The holding cells for the slaves were nothing like the Drej prison. The anxious prisoners clutched at the iron bars, grabbing at Korso and friends. Korso, Preed, and Stith searched each cell.

Korso stopped in front of a small, dark cell filled with humans and aliens. "Akima are you in there?" he called out.

Akima emerged. "If it isn't the captain," she said. "What kept you?" As she moved toward the door, an alien tried to catch her, but she knocked him unconscious.

Korso pulled out a gun and blasted the lock on her cell door. An alarm began to blare.

"Where's Cale?" Korso demanded.

"The Drej still have him," Akima said bitterly.

Korso couldn't believe it. "What?" he said.

Preed was getting nervous. "Do you suppose this alarm has gone unnoticed?" he asked.

Akima grabbed Stith's gun. "I'll give 'em something to notice," she said. "How about this?" She quickly moved from cell to cell blasting away at the locks. The prisoners stood there for a moment confused. They had been imprisoned so long they no idea what to do.

"Go on—get out of here," Akima shouted. "You're free!" She turned to the others. "Let's blow this dump."

With a mighty cheer, the prisoners realized their good fortune and came flooding out of their cells, nearly knocking over their saviors. The flood of human prisoners and the resulting mayhem gave the four an easy means for escape. They were able to make their way to the docking bay, slowly and calmly.

"Now let's go find Cale," Korso said.

CHAPTER 7

C ale leaped out of the way to avoid being seen by the Drej. That was a close one! He leaned over to see where he was and found that he was above the Drej queen's chamber. He leaned forward to hear her address her troops. Her words chilled him to the very bone.

"Prepare forces to destroy the *Titan*," she said in her frightening voice. "If the humans gain control of it, enact plans for elimination of the species."

Cale gulped. There was no time to lose! He immediately turned and sprinted down the hallway. Suddenly, he stopped dead in his tracks. A formation of Drej soldiers was marching right towards him! He ducked out of the way down a side hall. Without warning, Drej drones began to morph right in front of him. He immediately dove into another room. He looked around and discovered he was in a massive hangar, filled with stinger ships. Cale sprinted toward the nearest one and frantically reached up, trying to manipulate the energy of the stinger into morphing him inside. Finally, the stinger rose back up, with Cale at the helm. He placed his hands on the armrests, a look of fierce determination on his face. The ship was under his control. He joined a squadron of Drej stingers and lined up to exit the mothership. Cale's hands shook a little as he made his way into space.

As the ships moved away from the mothership, one lone stinger ship peeled off and rocketed away. It was Cale. He was finally able to stop holding his breath and breathe again. He was free!

Akima sat at the controls of the *Valkyrie*, scanning the heavens for a glimpse of Cale. "Do you see anything?" she asked worriedly. "It was really small like a cocoon or something…"

Gune shook his head grimly. "No, no nothing like that," he said. "No hmmm, I do see something," he said. "Ah, no just another Drej ship." He paused, realizing what he had just said. "Drej!" he shouted.

"What?" said Akima in a panic. "Where!"

Stith raced toward her weapons post. "I'm on it! I'm on it! I'm on it!" she shouted.

Akima picked up the intercom. "Korso, we have a problem," she said. "You'd better get up here."

Korso came running up the stairs as fast as he could. "I'm here! I'm here!" he said. "What's the problem?" He looked out the window at the Drej ship, which rocketed by. Then it turned back, heading right toward them.

"Stith!" Korso shouted in a panic. "Let's go!"

Stith was ready. "All right! All right!" she shouted. "I've locked on to him, sir!"

"Gune, look out for his buddies," warned Korso. Drej never traveled alone.

"There is only one," Gune said, sounding puzzled. "He is all alone. Just one."

Cale was getting impatient. He tapped a series of buttons on the stinger control panel, desperately trying to communicate with the *Valkyrie*. He knew that if he didn't reach them soon, his friends would mistakenly blast him right out of the sky.

"3...5...22..." Cale tapped out a code.

Gune heard this strange code broadcast over his communicator.

"3...5...22...74...11..." he said with a gasp. "Cale?"

But Stith was already blasting away at the stinger ship. "Die, Drej loser!" she shouted.

Cale's stomach sank. "Oh, no, don't shoot. Oh, guys, come on...it's me!" he groaned.

"It's Cale!" Gune yelled.

"Cale!" shouted Akima.

"Stith, hold your fire!" Korso thundered.

But it was too late. Stith had fired off another round. She cocked her head toward Korso.

"Oops?" she said.

Cale, meanwhile, dodged the stinger out of the way to avoid Stith's shots. He circled back around, looping over the *Valkyrie*. Everyone breathed a sigh of relief as they saw the Drej ship flying toward them.

"Akima! Open the cargo bay!" Korso commanded.

Cale drove the ship inside. He landed, a huge smile on his face. He was safe!

Akima raced into the cargo bay just as Cale stepped out of the ship. She stood at the top of the ladder, Cale at the bottom. They stared at each other joyously. "Cale!" Akima said, running down the stairs. When she reached the bottom, Cale swung her into the air. They both laughed out loud. He placed her down gently and they stared at each other, then stepped apart. They both had been certain they would never see one another alive again.

Their tender moment was broken when everyone else rushed to the cargo bay and peered down at them.

"The boy is not dead!" Gune shouted happily. "This is cause for happiness."

"Hmmm," said Preed.

"So, um, how did you escape?" asked Akima.

"He got lucky," answered Preed.

Korso made his way down the stairs, a huge grin on his face. "You know, we were just about to rescue you," he told Cale.

"Yeah?" said Cale. "Well, thanks."

"Anytime," Korso replied.

With a heavy heart, Cale told them what the Drej had done. "Look, they copied the map," he said. "I'm sure they're headed for the *Titan* now."

"They won't find it," Korso said in a sure voice. He turned and walked back up the stairs. "Stations, people," he commanded. Everyone made their way back. Akima and Cale brought up the rear.

"Uh, Akima," Cale said.

She stopped and turned toward him.

Cale shifted uncomfortably. "I...uh...what happened? How did you get back?"

"I got picked up with the trash," Akima explained, grinning ruefully. "Luckily, Korso got there before I ended up as the door prize in some alien freak show."

Cale couldn't help himself. He felt an overwhelming feeling of relief that Akima was safe. He reached out and tenderly brushed a lock of hair away from her face. "I guess I owe him one," he said, looking deep into her eyes. "You know," he continued, his voice choking up, "we both got really lucky back there. But the next time around..." his voice trailed off.

Just then, Korso turned around. "Cale, come on!" he shouted. "Gune needs a hand!"

Korso looked on as Gune studied the map on Cale's hand, once again trying to bend Cale's arm in impossible ways.

"Yes, the map is good," mused Gune. "The map is different. Yes, well, the map is clear now. Yes, it's very, very clear."

"Ow!" Cale groaned. "Take it easy!" He and Korso craned their necks to look.

Sure enough, the tattoo had changed.

Cale stared at it. "Hmmm. This outer marking is pulsing," he said.

Preed took a look. "Ahh…the distal phalangial meridian!" he announced.

Korso turned to Gune. "What do you make of it?" he asked.

Gune studied it again. "Past outer quadrant. These are the Ice Rings of Tigrin. Right here." He pointed to his revolving star map.

Preed nodded. "Easy to get lost in there," he said.

Korso agreed. "Good hiding place," he said. He turned to Cale. "Well, looks like we're one step ahead of the Drej after all, kid." He kept his eyes on Cale, addressing Gune. "You're sure about the location?" he asked.

"Yes, Captain," said Gune. "This time I'm absolutely sure."

Korso was pleased. "Well, I guess we're back in business," he said.

Gune giggled. He was quite pleased.

• • •

Cale walked onto the bridge of the ship alone, deep in thought. Things were happening so quickly. He sat in a chair and stared out the window into space. Suddenly, he was startled as something floated by the window. Then there was another. Then dozens of translucent creatures surrounded the ship. They were beautiful. He stared at them in wonder.

"Wake angels," a voice said. It was Korso. Cale hadn't noticed he was standing behind him. "They follow ships into deep space, glide on the energy wake. They're supposed to be good luck."

Cale stood and craned his neck to see them. They could certainly use some good luck right about now. The wake angels crossed in front of the *Valkyrie* playfully. "They're like ghosts," Cale said softly.

"Sit down," said Korso, pointing to the ship's controls. "Why don't you give them a run?"

Cale hesitated for a moment. "You sure about that?" he asked.

"Of course I'm sure," said Korso.

Cale was flattered. "Okay," he said. He took the wheel, a little unsteady at first. But under Korso's watchful eye, he soon evened out.

"Yeah, you got it," said Korso. "Open her up. Give these angels something to chase."

Cale laughed with pleasure. "All right," he said. "Try this, guys!" With a glance towards Korso, he fired the thrusters and gave the angels a chase they wouldn't soon forget. They dove down, and Cale followed. Next, he rolled away from them and began to climb, the angels close behind. They enveloped the ship in a silent rush. Cale drove the ship into the center of a brilliantly colored red and orange nebula, skillfully dodging enormous pillars of cosmic dust. The angels kept up the whole way.

"Uh, Cale, Cale watch it," stammered Korso nervously. "Be careful of the…"

"I've got it!" shouted Cale joyfully. "Woo-hoo!"

Once Korso saw that Cale had everything under control, he began to relax and enjoy the game. The angels kept pace throughout the entire ride. When Cale was through, he leveled the plane. The fragile-looking angels slowly peeled off and began to disperse. He watched them in awe, then turned to Korso gratefully. "Thank you," he said simply.

Korso nodded. "I knew you could handle this old bird."

Cale let out a breath. He struggled to find the words for what he wanted to say.

"No…I mean…for trying to find me." He turned around in his chair. "It's more than my father ever did," he said bitterly.

Korso stared at the boy. His pain was still raw, even fifteen years later. "Your father was a great man, Cale...he would have been proud of you."

"You really think so?" Cale said. For a moment he dropped his guard. The note of hope in his voice was heart-breaking. He stood and began to walk down the stairs.

"Trust me," said Korso.

"Thanks...thanks," Cale said. Then in a lower tone he said, "You know, I miss him."

Korso sighed. "Me too," he said.

CHAPTER 8

Cale sat on the edge of his bunk, thinking over the events of the day. And what a day it had been! Just then, he heard a noise coming from out in the hallway. Curious, he leaned forward. His door slid open, and for a moment, he had to squint in the blinding light. Then as his eyes focused, he could see that two Drej soldiers were silhouetted in the doorway. Before Cale could even open up his mouth to scream, they opened fire on him, blasting him back against the bunk.

The next thing Cale knew, he awoke in a cold sweat, shivering. Even though it was only a nightmare, his heart was still racing.

Unable to sleep, he rose from his bed and walked down the hall to a nearby door.

He knocked on it lightly, hoping the occupant was still awake. "Akima? Akima?" He slid the door open.

Akima jumped, clutching a towel around her. He stood sheepishly in the doorway. "Oh, uh…sorry…uh…I…" he said awkwardly.

"In or out?" asked Akima.

"Huh?" said Cale, confused. "Oh! Uh, in!" he said. He stepped inside and closed the door behind him.

"Uh, what's going on?" Cale asked. "Do you know why we stopped?"

"Pit stop at the Drifter Colony for the basics," Akima explained. "Food, water, shield-core reactant." She walked into a small room and the door slid shut. She began getting dressed. Cale could see her silhouette through the glass. Nervously, he looked away. He half-listened to her talk, fidgeting with the collection of Earth relics on a small table. A baseball. Some postcards. A comic book.

"Hmm, listen, I need to talk to you," Cale said. "Um, I…" He cleared his throat and changed the subject. "Where did you get all this junk?" He picked up the baseball and rolled it around in his hands.

Akima, fully dressed, stepped over to Cale as she toweled her hair dry. "It's not junk," she said. "Why don't you come with me? I'll show you." She grabbed the baseball and carefully placed it back on the table.

Akima and Cale were loaded down with boxes of food and water they would use to trade with the Drifter Colonists. Cale was puzzled. "So we're going to offer this stuff for more of that…" he searched for the word, "earth junk?"

Akima shook her head. "Don't you get it Cale? That junk is all that's left of the place we came from. It reminds us of what it means to have a home."

Cale looked away. "Well, I don't know about that. I've never had one."

Just then Korso's voice interrupted them. But this wasn't the strong, brave Korso that Akima and Cale knew. This was a furious, dark Korso that neither one of them had ever seen before.

"Who do you think you are?" the captain thundered. "You think this is some kind of game? We had a deal, darn it! How dare you try to cut me out like that?"

Akima and Cale stopped in their tracks. Who had gotten Korso so angry? They were floored when they realized that their captain was addressing the Drej queen, whose holographic image filled the room with blue light.

"We will do as we please in order to ensure the *Titan's* retrieval," the queen replied, unemotionally.

Korso was furious. "Yeah? Do as you please and guess what? You'll retrieve nothing! You don't have the whole map. The kid's got it and I've got the kid. So you keep the drones off my tail, or so help me, *I'll rip his heart out.*"

The queen snarled angrily. Korso punched his wrist communicator, ending their conversation.

Cale and Akima stood in the doorway, unable to move. They were devastated. Korso, their trusted captain, was a traitor!

"Cale, come on!" Akima finally said. The two stepped back into the shadows, about to make their escape, when Preed stepped forward, a gun in his hand. It was aimed right at Cale's heart.

"Going somewhere?" he asked in a mocking tone. He pushed Cale and Akima into Korso's room. "Look what I found!" Preed said with a cackle. "Two little birdies itching to fly!"

Korso stared, the mixture of guilt and anger he was feeling written all over his face. "How long were they standing there?" he asked.

Akima lifted her chin in defiance. "Long enough," she spat out.

Cale was devastated. "You lied," he said miserably. "Everything you said…everything you told me…"

"Not everything," said Korso coldly, pointing his finger in Cale's face. "Your father hid a ship. Then the Drej killed him. All because he couldn't face the truth."

"What's the truth?" Cale asked bitterly.

"That the human race is out of gas," explained Korso. "It's circling the drain. It's finished. The only thing that matters is grabbing what you can before someone else beats you to it."

Cale shook his head, taking a step back. "No, I don't believe that…"

Korso narrowed his eyes and glared at Cale. "Then you're even more like your father than I thought. You're a fool!"

Filled with blind rage, Cale lunged at Korso, knocking him to the ground. As they wrestled, Korso, the older and stronger of the two, quickly got the upper hand and punched Cale right in the face. Akima was about to jump in when Preed leapt forward and held her back.

"Cale!" she shouted.

Just then, Cale reached out and grabbed a glass container. He smashed it in Korso's face, giving him the opportunity he needed

"Akima! Come on!" yelled Cale. He jumped up. Akima wrenched herself free from Preed's grip and the two began to run down the hall.

"Stop them!" shouted Korso. "Stay on them! I'll lock it down!"

"Hurry!" called Akima.

They ran as fast as they could. But their only means of escape—a doorway that led to an airlock that would take them to the Drifter Colony—was closing before their eyes. They dove for it, scrambling under it just in time. Breathing hard, they sprinted down the long airlock. Preed fell to the floor and began shooting under the door. One of his bullets found its mark and Akima went down. Cale scooped her up into his arms and kept running until he reached the door that would take them to the Drifter Colony. He looked down at her. She was breathing—but just barely. Cale looked out the small window of the door, across the airlock at Korso. His eyes were dark with hate.

Korso stared back, then turned to Preed. "Let's go," he said. "We've got a ship to find."

Cale watched them go, then returned his look to Akima, cradling her head gently. She coughed once, then slipped into unconsciousness.

Back on the *Valkyrie*, Gune and Stith greeted Preed and Korso. "Let's get airborne," snapped Korso. "Now!"

"Where are Cale and Akima?" Stith asked innocently.

"They're not coming," answered Korso in a clipped tone.

"Why not?" Stith pressed.

Korso spun around, barely containing his anger. "Because they're afraid," he said.

"Afraid?" asked Stith with disbelief. "What exactly are they afraid of?"

Korso stalked toward her, his face red with rage. "They're afraid of what might happen if my command is ever questioned!" he thundered. "Get it?"

"Got it," Stith replied, not getting it at all.

Korso whipped around and faced Gune. "You got a problem with that?"

Gune shrugged. As Korso and Preed stalked out of the room, Stith and Gune stared at each other.

"Why they not say good-bye to Gune?" Gune said sadly. Stith gently patted her friend on the head. She didn't know the answer. All she knew was that something was wrong. Very wrong.

CHAPTER 9

In the village square, an elderly Asian woman led Cale to a stone table and indicated that he should lay Akima down. A group gathered and watched solemnly. The woman began barking orders. "You go get doctor!" she commanded to an onlooker. A couple of the colonists removed their shabby coats and covered Akima's still figure. The woman turned to someone else and said something in a language Cale couldn't understand.

"What did you tell him?" Cale asked curiously.

"I ask him to bring corn liquor," the old woman replied.

Akima struggled to speak. "No, really I don't need it," she said weakly.

"Not for you," explained the old woman with a laugh. "For boy," she said, motioning toward the ashen Cale.

"Me?" said Cale.

"He pass out soon!" responded the old woman.

Akima gave Cale a weak smile. He laughed sheepishly and touched her face. He stared down, unable to take his eyes off her. But he felt the presence of the colonists around him. They had come forward to offer their help, support, even the tattered clothes off their backs. Cale took a deep breath. Maybe Tek was right. Maybe there was something to this human solidarity thing after all. For the first time in fifteen years, Cale realized that he really wasn't all alone out there after all.

• • •

Later, Cale stood, looking out an enormous window at the stars that hung in the sky above the Drifter Colony. Akima walked up to him, wrapped in a blanket.

"Hey, Sleeping Beauty," said Cale in a teasing tone.

"How long was I out?" Akima asked.

"Not long," said Cale, placing his hands on his hips. "A few hours."

Akima stared out the window. "Korso…and Preed. I can't believe it. How long before they reach the *Titan*?"

Cale was firm. "They won't. We're gonna beat them to it. Akima, we're gonna stop them."

"Was I seriously injured back there or something?" Akima asked. "Because, funny, I thought you just said, 'We're gonna stop them.'"

"That's right," Cale said decidedly.

Akima spoke, the voice of reason. She began to tick off the reasons that this was a ridiculous plan. "Cale, we're in the middle of nowhere, there's just the two of us, and oh yeah—we don't have a ship!"

Cale smiled. "Oh, we've got a ship," he said mysteriously.

Akima snorted. "Really? I'd like to see this ship."

"Okay," said Cale. He grabbed her by the shoulders and turned her around to look out the window. The Drifter Colony was made of ship hulls. On the edge was a large rocket clearly in disrepair.

"Oh, no," Akima whispered under her breath.

"Oh, yes," said Cale.

$$\bullet \ \bullet \ \bullet$$

The rocket was the home of the mayor of the Drifter Colony. "Well, she's been a great house," the mayor said. "But I don't think she'll fly."

Cale leaned forward and popped open a rocket panel. He poked around for a moment. "Well, she's still got her ionic vacuum drive," he said. "Those never drain."

"This thing's a wreck!" Akima protested.

Cale nodded. "I can fix it," he said assuredly. "But do you think…"

She looked at him with disdain. "Don't worry, I can fly it," she said.

• • •

After tons of hard work—welding, repairing, cleaning, fueling, and jerry-rigging the ship—they were finally done. There were colonists perched on platforms, prepping the rocket for take off. Akima and Cale knew that they never could have completed the task without the colonists' help. On the ship's upper platform, Akima watched closely as Cale made the final adjustments. He leaned forward and wiped a layer of dust off the side, revealing its name: the *Phoenix*. And like the mythic bird, it too would rise from the ashes. Or at least that's what everyone hoped.

Cale looked down at the colonists and flashed them the thumbs up sign. The colonists cheered.

In the cockpit, Akima smoothly ran through the pre-flight sequence, hitting buttons and flicking switches.

"Well, we're good to go," Cale announced.

"Let's hope she starts," warned Akima. The countdown began. 10…9…8…7…

"Oh, she'll start," Cale assured her.

"Yeah, right," said Akima.

3…2…1…0. Nothing.

Akima gave Cale a look.

"She'll start!" Cale insisted. "Uh, I'd lean back if I were you."

The engine let out a weak sputter. "Should I get out and push?" Akima asked wryly.

There was silence for a moment, then suddenly, the jet engine roared to life with an incredibly large belch of fire and energy.

"Whoa!" Akima shouted as she was thrown back in her seat.

Cale laughed happily. "I told ya!" he said.

The colonists cheered, taking a step backwards as the *Phoenix* started to lift. As Cale gave her an I-told-you-so look, Akima rolled her eyes. Grabbing the controls, she turned to him and said, "Okay, you did *your* job, now let me do *mine*." She guided the shaking ship past the hull of the Drifter Colony—perilously close to hitting it. Cale sucked in his breath sharply. He knew Akima was an expert pilot, but this was getting a little too close for comfort!

Her brow furrowed in concentration, Akima nimbly guided the *Phoenix* through the maze of structures. Soon they were free.

. . .

Back on the *Valkyrie*, the tension could have been cut with a knife. Gune steered the ship while Stith and Preed nervously scanned the monitors for a glimpse of the *Titan*. Korso nervously paced back and forth behind them, pausing every couple of minutes to look out at the stars. He was tense. Very tense.

"Those darn collisons keep slowing us down!" he complained. "So where is it?"

Preed spoke up. "My scanners are picking up a veritable cornucopia of…nothing!"

Korso stalked up to Preed angrily. "Just find it!" he shouted. He turned to Gune. "Gune, are you sure about the map?"

Gune looked up at him, a hurt expression in his huge eyes. "You give me map, I follow map," he said. "Map takes us here, what more can Gune do?" he said with a shrug.

This time Preed lost it. "If Professor Screw-Loose over there led us off course, I'm going to…"

Stith interrupted him before he could finish his threat. "Hold it," she said, her eyes on her scanner.

Korso leaned forward. "What is it?" he asked excitedly.

"A ship," Stith replied. "Three keks east."

"Drej?" asked Preed worriedly.

"No," Stith answered. "Human craft. Heading for the break zone. Moving fast."

"How fast?" asked Korso.

Stith studied the screen for a moment. "I'd say recklessly fast," was her answer.

Korso nodded. "Akima," he said knowingly. He looked at Preed, his gaze an equal mix of surprise and concern.

Gune brightened. Their friends were found! "Ah good, Akima, Cale!" he said. "I hail on communicator."

"No hailing!" commanded Korso. "Just follow them…"

Gune was confused, but did as he was commanded. He ran through a sequence of switches, and the *Valkyrie* shuddered and began to turn around.

"Okay, I follow," he said. But he knew they were headed into dangerous territory. "But I plot new route through safer quadrant."

That's when Korso lost it. Snarling, he knocked Gune out of the way and seized the controls.

"We're going to follow them!" he thundered. "And we'll run silent."

Gune and Stith stared at each other worriedly. Something strange was going on and neither one of them liked it one bit.

CHAPTER 10

Gune was right. The quadrant was indeed dangerous, a minefield of jagged ice at every turn. It was strange, yet eerily beautiful. Huge star-shaped crystals crashed together around them in explosions of glass-like ice. But the *Phoenix* managed to gracefully make its way through, narrowly missing massive chunks of spiraling ice. Akima steered the way silently, concentrating hard. "The reflections are throwing my readings off," she said softly.

Distractedly, Cale rubbed the hand with the map on it. He looked down and noticed that it was pulsating faintly. "Uh, Akima," he said. "I think we're getting closer."

Akima nodded, then leaned forward as she caught sight of something from the corner of her eye. In the ice, she could see the reflection of a very familiar spacecraft.

"Cale!" she exclaimed. "It's Korso! He's right behind us!"

Cale looked out the window and saw the reflection, too.

"We've got to lose him!" he said.

Akima leaned forward and began flipping switches. "You've got it!" she said, trying to speed up. But something was wrong.

"What's happening?" Cale asked in a panicked voice.

"I don't know!" said Akima. "I think the vacuum drive lost its power!"

An overwhelming feeling of dread came over Cale. They were close, and yet so far. "Oh no!" he said. He leaned forward and peered out into the mist. He thought he heard the *Valkyrie* getting closer. "You hear that?" he said to Akima.

"We've got to get out of here," she replied, punching some buttons.

"Stith, where are they?" Korso yelled.

Stith was getting frustrated. "I can't get a reading!" she responded.

"There is too much ice," said Gune. "Too much interference."

"Captain!" shouted Preed. When the mist parted he could see that they were headed straight toward an enormous ice crystal.

"Whoa!" yelled Korso, yanking at the controls. They narrowly missed it.

Akima turned to Cale. "The vacuum drives never drain, huh?" she said, mocking him.

"What about the thrusters?" suggested Cale.

Akima shook her head. "How far can we get on thrusters?" she asked.

Just then two huge ice crystals crashed together right in front of them in an explosion of ice fragments. One hit their ship.

"I think we'd better find out now," said Cale.

"Roger that," said Akima. "We need those engines. Hurry!"

Cale disappeared downstairs. Akima could hardly sit still as she waited. She looked out the window. "Uh-oh!" she shouted. "Korso found us!"

"Where is he?" called Cale, working away.

With the reflections all around them, Akima saw him coming from many different directions. "I-I don't know!" she yelled.

• • •

Preed smiled. "We found them, Captain," he said.

Korso nodded. "Until they make their move, we stay here." He folded his arms across his chest.

• • •

Just then, Cale came upstairs. "The engines should be okay now," he said breathlessly.

"Let's give 'em a shot," replied Akima. She fired the ship to life and began, once again, to cautiously make her way through the exploding ice crystals.

•••

Preed studied the *Phoenix*. "They're moving out," he said. "I think," he added uncertainly. The ship was reflected in so many different places!

Korso stared out the window. "Where the heck are they?" he asked.

•••

From their new position, Akima spotted the *Valkyrie* at the end of a long ice tunnel. She came to a stop. "I can't move!" she said. "They'll see us!"

But Cale had a plan. With all the reflections, this was the perfect way to escape. He grabbed her wrist. "Maybe that's exactly what we want!" he exclaimed. Akima moved the ship forward again, and an explosion of haphazardly shifting ice crystals just missed them once again.

•••

"They're right in front of us!" Gune shouted.

"You're not gonna get past me, kid," Korso vowed.

"There, Captain!" shouted Preed, pointing.

"Yeah," said Korso. "But which one?" They all stared out into the vast ice landscape as dozens of different reflections bounced off the ice. Which was the real one?

"Closer," said Gune. "They're getting closer!"

"There she is, Captain!" said Preed. Everyone stared. But it was just a reflection that became distorted as the real ship passed by, no one knew where. "No, there!" called Preed, pointing again.

"Which one?" Korso shouted, raising his fists in frustration.

• • •

Meanwhile, the real ship passed behind them, unnoticed. Akima turned to Cale. "I think we're going to get away with this!" she said, unbelievingly.

"You may be right!" Cale replied.

• • •

"Look! They're behind us now!" Gune shouted in confusion.

The *Phoenix* saw its chance and took off, speeding forward as a series of crystals exploded into one another. But the *Valkyrie* was not so nimble. In the confusion, the ice began to crash around it, trapping them in an ice prison. Korso was furious.

"Ready lasers!" he thundered. In a brilliant red flash, the *Valkyrie* blasted itself free.

"We're clear!" cried Korso, grabbing the controls. "Don't lose them!"

The ship surged forward, narrowly missing a huge shower of jagged ice shards.

The race was on. Akima sped forward, as fast as her ship would go. But the *Valkyrie* was gaining on them. There was only one thing left to do. She bit her lower lip and steered the ship into a dangerous cluster of ice crystals about to collide.

Cale looked up and panicked. "Ice!" he yelled. "Turn back!"

Akima never blinked. "Uh-uh, no way," she replied.

"We'll never make it through!" he shouted.

Akima's voice was calm. "We don't have a choice," she replied and entered the dangerous terrain. It was a desperate race through the shattering ice, Korso right on their tail. It was all Cale could do to keep from covering his eyes. But in the confusion and the shards of spiraling ice, they lost him. Finally, they were safe.

"Let's not do that again," Akima said wryly.

They both breathed a sigh of relief. Then Akima turned to Cale. "So, uh, your hand said this way, huh?"

Cale shrugged. "Oh, yeah, I guess so," he said. "It's not a real exact science."

"Great," said Akima, pointing up ahead. "Well, could you maybe ask the hand if it's a left or a right up ahead?"

Cale took a deep breath. "I'd definitely say left," he said. "No, maybe right."

"Cale," said Akima in a warning tone.

"Yeah, definitely right," he decided.

The right tunnel led them to an enormous cavernous space. Up ahead loomed more huge ice crystals. "Hold it, look there," said Cale.

"I don't see anything," replied Akima.

"The reflections!" Cale shouted. "Akima turn around. Turn around!"

Akima turned the ship. "Steady, that's it," said Cale.

It was the *Titan*. The huge bronze orb floated silently in space. It was the ship that Sam Tucker had given his life for, the ship that so many people had pinned their only hopes of a future on. It was here.

Akima gasped. "Have you ever seen anything like it?" she asked.

Cale smiled faintly, remembering a day, long ago. "Just once," he said simply.

The *Phoenix* slowly approached the massive ship, stopping at her docking port.

Cale and Akima stepped onto the ship. Lights along the floor flashed on, illuminating the way for them. The lights led to a platform in the middle of the ship. It was cold onboard and their breath made big white puffs in the air.

"What exactly are we looking for?" asked Akima.

"This ship's going to help us save humankind," replied Cale.

But he hadn't answered her question. "What exactly are we looking for?" Akima asked again.

"Not a clue," admitted Cale.

Cale stared at the rows of containers and vials that lined the walls. His brow furrowed, he leaned over, picking up a vial and inspecting its label. "DNA coding," he said. "Mammal. *Tursiops truncatus*…the bottle-nosed dolphin." He thought for a moment. "These are animals," he announced. "Or they will be…"

Akima leaned over and read another vial. "Leopard, elephant, oh…butterfly!" she said with delight. "It's all here!"

Cale looked around in wonder, then spotted something and let out a gasp. He raced up to the platform in the middle of the room.

Akima looked around. Where did he go? "Cale?" she said worriedly.

"I'm over here!" he called.

Cale was at the control platform of the ship. He could hardly believe his eyes—it was his toy from that day long ago on the river. His father had taken it with him to remember Cale by. He picked up the toy and turned it around and around in his hands, remembering. His eyes filled with tears as he recollected the day he and his father built the toy. When Cale closed his eyes, he could see the two of them sitting side-by-side, putting it together. "Dad," he whispered.

Cale snapped out of his reverie as Akima approached him. He looked down and saw an activation cone. Without being told, he knew that this was where his ring belonged. He slipped it off his finger and placed it over the top of the cone. It was a perfect fit. He waited to see what would happen...

And floor by floor, the *Titan's* lights all switched on. It was an enormous space—larger than either of them had realized. Cale and Akima looked around them in amazement.

• • •

Outside, the *Valkyrie* docked next to the *Phoenix*. Stith and Gune walked down the stairs where they found Korso and Preed checking their weapons.

"I'm ready to go, Captain," Stith announced.

Korso thought quickly. "You two stay here," he said. "Preed and I can wrap this up."

Stith was confused. As the weapons expert, she always went along with her captain.

"But…"

Without a word, Korso turned on his heel and left. Preed handed Stith a communication device. "Here, hold on to this," he said with an evil smile, "in case there's any trouble."

Stith took the device while Gune looked on suspiciously. Preed exited the ship leaving the hatchway door open. "Hmmm," said Gune. "No, no, no, no." Something was wrong, very wrong. Gune couldn't explain it—he just knew. He stared after the departing Preed.

As Korso and Preed walked onboard the *Titan*, Korso turned to Preed. "Those two are becoming a problem," he said. "We need to take care of it."

Preed laughed cruelly. "I'm one step ahead of you," he said.

• • •

Stith and Gune stood inside the *Valkyrie*. Stith shook her head in confusion. "Watch the ship," Gune complained. "I *always* watch the ship!"

Stith shook her head. "I don't know, but this just doesn't feel right."

"I wanna go!" Gune said. "I want to *go!*"

Stith looked unsure. "The captain said stay!"

"It's *Captain* I don't trust," Gune whispered, as if Korso was still within earshot.

"Mmmm," said Stith. "You know, you may be right," she said. "Come on." They both turned to leave. That's when the communicator beeped.

Stith switched it on. "Stith here," she said.

"Stith!" said Preed. "Is Gune right there with you?"

"Yeah," said Stith.

"Then tell him good-bye for me, won't you?" said Preed.

Stith stared at the communicator in disbelief. "What?" she said.

Finally realizing what was going on, Gune snatched the communicator from Stith's wrist and ran down the hall with it. Just as he threw it into the air, the device blew into smithereens, blasting them both backwards in a wave of fire and debris.

The smoke cleared and Stith staggered over to Gune. She was wounded, but she would be okay. "Gune?" said Stith. She spotted him pinned beneath a slab of the ship's paneling and she wrenched it off him. "Gune are you all right?" she asked anxiously.

Gune looked up. "I'm all right for business," he managed to say.

Stith's heart sank. "Gune..." she said.

"I'll just take a little nap," said Gune, closing his eyes. "Since I'm so very sleepy." He stopped moving. Stith brought her head close to Gune's. "I'll come back for you," she said. When she raised her head, there was a murderous gleam in her eyes. She would avenge for her friend.

• • •

Unseen by anyone, the Drej mothership approached the ice rings. She too, was on her way to the *Titan.* Time was running out!

• • •

Inside the *Titan*, Cale and Akima approached the control platform and looked out over the expanse of the illuminated *Titan* interior. Cale's ring, around the tip of the activation cone, began to glow and pulse. Behind the two, a figure began to materialize above the central hologram projector on the control platform. A celestial light emanated from its beam.

"Cale," said the oh-so-familiar voice.

The twenty-year-old Cale turned around, but the voice that emerged from his lips was that of the five-year-old boy who had been left behind. "Dad?" he said softly. He stepped forward to stand before his father.

"If this message has been activated," said Sam Tucker, "then I have died before finding you."

Cale stared at his father sadly.

"Oh, I wish I could see you," Sam said. "I wish I could be there."

Cale's heart ached. If only this were his real father standing before him, not a hologram!

"I don't know if you'll ever forgive me for leaving," Sam continued. "I hope you understand that I had to. I had to keep you safe…" He paused for a moment. "Cale, this ship has the power to create a planet...to create a new home..."

Cale and Akima stared at each other in astonishment. This was remarkable news!

Sam continued. "Your ring would have activated the transformation sequence, but the *Titan's* power cells were drained in the escape. They are unable to fuel the transformation."

Cale and Akima both sighed in frustration.

"It is up to you to restore their power, after that, the procedure is simple..." Cale leaned forward to hear, but a laser blast suddenly punched a hole in the hologram generator and Sam Tucker disintegrated. Cale and Akima whipped around to see Korso standing in the stairway. "He always did talk too much," said Korso cruelly.

Akima pulled out her weapon. A second laser blast sent her gun flying out of her hand. Preed, his gun drawn, was standing next to Korso.

Korso approached Cale and Akima. "Korso, don't do this. This ship is all we have left—doesn't that mean anything to you?"

Korso sneered. "Sorry kid," he said. "The world blowing up changes a man."

Cale interrupted, "Look the Drej…"

Korso shrugged. "See, you can't beat the Drej. No one can—they're pure energy. Face it, Cale. You've lost."

Preed stepped forward. "Actually, you all have," he said, cocking his gun and resting it against the back of Korso's head. "Captain, if you'll relieve yourself of your firearm…"

Korso could not believe his ears. "You backstabbing…"

"Well, I learned it from the best," Preed said with a smirk.

There was nothing else for him to do. Korso held up his gun, and Preed took it, throwing it over the side of the platform.

"But it wasn't the money the Drej were offering," Preed continued. "It was the health plan that came with it—they'd let me live, provided I kill all of you before they get here." He paused for dramatic emphasis. "They should be here shortly."

Preed smiled at Cale, all the while keeping his guns trained on Akima and Korso. Preed did not notice as Korso reached over and snatched Cale's ring from the cone-shaped activator.

Akima spoke up. "Preed, you can't trust the Drej," she said.

Preed sighed. "Stop!" he said. "There's nothing more tiresome than last-minute heroics," he complained.

Korso took the chance to dive over a railing to the narrow ledge below. Preed turned, distracted, which gave Akima the chance to jump him. Preed opened fire on Korso, but his aim was thrown off by Akima's knee to his stomach. Preed gave her a wicked blow with an elbow to the head, and Cale jumped on him. Preed knocked Cale to the ground. He looked around wildly. Where was Korso?

Cale tried to rise to his feet, but the wind was knocked out of him and he just couldn't do it. Preed whipped around, pulled out his blaster, and fired at Cale. With his last remaining ounce of strength, Cale rolled behind a bank of machinery and managed to just miss getting hit.

Preed laughed an evil laugh. "Ahhh! Hide and seek!" he cackled. "Or should we play search and destroy?" He didn't see Korso sneaking up the stairs behind him. Cale did and shouted out a warning. "Preed!" he yelled.

Preed spun around and fired. At the very same time, Korso jumped, slinging one of his arms around Preed's neck and snapping it. Preed slumped lifelessly to the floor. Korso stood over Preed's lifeless body, and after a moment, kicked it down the stairs.

Korso turned around to get the shock of his life. Cale now pointed Preed's gun at him! "Give me that ring!" Cale demanded.

Korso shook his head. "You're not going to shoot me, kid," he said in a level voice.

Instead of an answer, Cale directed a blast at Korso's boots and he took a step backwards. But Cale's victory was momentary—Korso dropkicked the gun right out of Cale's hand.

Cale jumped Korso and the two rolled around on the floor, a blur of fists and feet. The ring was knocked out of Korso's hand and they both toppled backward over a railing and fell onto a catwalk. But it couldn't hold their weight and collapsed. Without thinking about what he was doing, Cale instinctively grabbed Korso's arm to save him.

Cale stared for a moment, unsure of what to do. Korso was his enemy! But he couldn't watch him fall to his death. "Hold on!" Cale yelled in a panic. But his grip was slipping. He struggled to support Korso who dangled in midair.

Korso looked right into Cale's eyes. "You can let go, kid," he said. "I wouldn't blame you." He began to slip, but Cale still struggled to keep his grip.

"No, I'm not going to let go," he said firmly. But the weight was too much for Cale to handle. Korso's arm slipped out of his grip and the captain plummeted down, down, down.

"Korso!" Cale screamed.

But miraculously, just before Korso hit the bottom, he managed to reach out and grabbed a dangling strand of cable. He safely bobbed up and down mere inches from some jutting reactor spikes. Korso stared at the spikes unbelievingly.

As Cale swung himself over the railing, Akima and Stith raced over to see if he was okay.

"Anything broken?" Stith asked.

"You okay?" Akima asked him.

"Yeah," said Cale. He leaned over to snatch his father's ring off the floor. Suddenly, he, Akima, and Stith lost their balance as the *Titan* shook. They were being attacked by enemy fire.

It was the Drej mothership. "Disarm the *Titan* and remove any means of escape!" Queen Drej thundered. A dozen stingers broke off from the Drej armada and made a beeline for the *Titan*.

Cale began fiddling with one of the *Titan's* computers. "Let's not panic," he said in a semi-panicked voice.

"We have to get out of here before the Drej arrive!" Akima shouted.

Cale took a deep breath. He had a plan. "No, I think we're going to stay right here," he said.

Akima stared at the radar screen. "Right here is about to be blown to bits!" she yelled. What was Cale doing?

Cale was still fixed on the computer. "This could be a good thing," he muttered.

Akima watched him in disbelief. "Come on, Cale!" she yelled.

"Wait, wait, we can make this work!" Cale insisted. "What did Korso say about the Drej?"

"That you can't beat them!" said Akima.

Cale nodded, putting it all together. "Right, because they're pure energy. If I can re-route the system to use Drej energy, then that would start the reactor." He began to run through the routine in the computer console. "The energy relays are linked to these circuit breakers," he said. "So, this should do it." He indicated the computer screen, where circuit breaker #1 was locking into place.

"Yes!" said Cale.

Akima did not look convinced. "Are you sure this will work?" she asked

Cale pointed to the computer screen again, which showed circuit breaker #2 also locking into place. They both smiled. But their smiles faded as the malfunction lights began to flash for circuit breaker #3.

"Darn it!" Cale exploded. He shook his head then turned to Akima. "I can fix this. I need to get outside. Can you and Stith cover me?"

Without even waiting for an answer, Cale ran down a flight of stairs. "I just need a little time," he said,

Stith and Akima ran over to load up on weapons. "How much time?" Akima asked.

"Uh, a few hours," said Cale.

"What can you do in a few minutes?" asked Stith.

Cale shook his head and climbed into an elevator, rocketing upward to an airlock opening onto the hull.

• • •

The Drej stingers were getting closer. They blasted through the ice crystals in their path as Akima and Stith watched them approach on their radar screens. Akima's hands were shaking and Stith's breath was coming in jagged gasps. But they were ready. The crew grabbed their gun turrets and locked on to the incoming ships.

"Here they come!" shouted Akima.

"Not if I can help it!" Stith yelled.

Just then, Cale emerged from the airlock in a spacesuit and mag boots, clutching a toolkit in his hand.

"Cale! You're a sitting duck out there!" Akima wailed into the microphone.

"Come on!" yelled Stith, trying to get her to concentrate on the oncoming Drej ships.

Cale had just leaned down to work on the base of the cannon when two Drej stingers whipped past him. Spotting him, they opened fire. Akima was right. He was a sitting duck. Bursts of plasma exploded at Cale's feet. He dove to avoid a second round of Drej fire.

Stith turned and coolly squared the attacking ship in her sights. Letting out a blood-curdling war whoop, she blasted the ship out of the sky. The massive fireball that resulted took the other stinger down with it. However, the ship began its nosedive, directly toward the *Titan*.

Cale stared in shock and disbelief. The ship was headed straight for him! "Oh no!" he screamed. He ran, dove, and cartwheeled across the hull in his desperate attempt to avoid being crushed by the crashing ship. As it crash-landed, it slid to a bone-crunching stop, pinning Cale to the hull. Cale squirmed and tried to wrench himself free. But it was no use—he was pinned to the ship like a delicate butterfly. And there was no way for him to move without ripping the fabric of his spacesuit. Now he was a sitting duck—for real.

"Cale, are you all right?" asked Akima in a panicked voice.

Cale wasn't quite sure how to answer that. "Uh, I'm hanging!" he replied.

Akima turned to Stith. "Who's outside with Cale?" she asked.

Trapped, Cale looked up and saw—Korso. His heart sank. The captain had him where he wanted him. This was it. It was strange, he didn't feel scared—only sad, terribly sad. They had been so close...and now it was all over.

"Hi kid," said Korso.

"It's Korso!" Akima said with a gasp.

Cale shook his head ruefully. "You'll never get a cleaner shot Korso," he said.

Korso nodded solemnly. He aimed the gun, pulled the trigger, and BLAM! hit a Drej pilot just emerging from the fallen stinger. A second blast destroyed the stinger's nose, setting Cale free.

"Maybe we can beat them after all!" Korso said.

Cale was speechless.

Korso pointed to the stinger wreckage, as yet another Drej pilot scrambled free. Korso shot him too, and began to aim his gun at the stingers passing overheard.

He turned to Cale. "Go ahead," he said. "I'll cover you!" He smiled at the "kid." Cale smiled back. "Yeah! Yeah! Right!" he said excitedly.

As Akima, Stith, and now Korso blasted away at the oncoming stingers, Cale sprinted for the damaged breaker and floated down to it. First he tried a manual overdrive sequence—which merely triggered sounds of a further shutdown. "Oh great!" Cale moaned. Next he tried to force the two sides of the enormous breaker together. But they would not budge.

"This is *not* a problem!" Cale announced. "I can fix this!"

• • •

The Drej queen issued her final command. "Destroy the ice shield that protects the *Titan*," she said.

• • •

"Let's do this!" Akima shouted.

Stith took out a wave of attacking stingers, but she was out of bullets. Her gun clicked uselessly. "Well guys, it's been fun," she said. But before her and Akima's unbelieving eyes, the stingers began to withdraw!

"They're leaving!" said Akima.

Korso, too, noticed the retreating Drej. "Uh-oh, we've got a problem!" he said. He jumped down to where Cale was frantically working on breaker #3.

"Go!" Korso shouted. "They're joining the mothership!"

"But the breaker!" Cale argued.

"Cale," said Korso. "She's preparing to fire!"

Cale stared at Korso. "You can't stay out here!" he protested.

"I'll take care of it. You man the activator," said Korso firmly. When Cale didn't move, he threw him forcefully against the wall. "Would you get the heck out of here!" he yelled.

Cale stared. If Korso stayed out here he would not survive. Despite what Korso had done, he couldn't leave his friend alone. Then he heard Akima's voice in his ear, "Cale where are you?" she asked worriedly.

Korso looked into Cale's eyes. "Go," he said. "It's better this way."

Cale nodded sadly, and Korso smiled at him. Then he floated up and outside, scrambling back to the ship, dodging fire from the few remaining stinger ships.

"Korso, how's it coming partner?" he called out.

Korso was wounded, but smiled in spite of the pain. "Nearly got it," he said.

Cale dodged the plasma explosions, then tripped and stumbled to the ground, right into the line of fire of an approaching stinger. It looked like he was a goner! Just then the attacking stinger exploded! Cale struggled to his feet, stunned to see the *Valkyrie* roaring past him, with Gune at the controls!

"I finished my nap!" shouted Gune.

"Gune!" cried Stith, fighting back tears. He was alive!

Gune laughed away. "Bomb strong, Gune stronger!" he said. "Now I blow up ships. Yes!" He began to fire away at the remaining stinger ships.

• • •

Cale raced inside, peeled off the suit, and threw himself into the elevator. He pulled off his ring, willing the elevator to speed up. "Come on, faster! Faster!"

• • •

The queen Drej had reassembled the remaining Drej stingers into the large laser-firing formation that had annihilated Earth fifteen years earlier.

"Lock in the *Titan*," she said. "Now we finish it."

The laser gun glowed and the mighty beam began to make its way toward its target.

He was out of time. Korso had tried everything else and there was only one thing left to do. He ran towards the breaker, his blaster clutched in his hands. He jammed it between the breaker's receptacle, completing the circuit. But there was no more time. Korso had knowingly sacrificed himself. He howled, triumphant, as the Drej's deadly beam consumed him in a blast of blue energy.

• • •

Cale jumped off the elevator and raced to the control unit. He shoved his ring on the activation cone. There was a huge zap.

The Drej energy traveled from the tower through the circuit breaker, reaching the reactor gun and igniting its laser beam. Three laser beams of Drej energy converged and moved down towards the *Titan's* genesis reactor. As it locked in, the reactor began to spin and glow. The ring control began to turn in a clockwise direction. Cale grinned with satisfaction as a positive warm-colored energy began to emit from the genesis reactor ring.

• • •

The queen Drej had been watching the *Titan* with satisfaction, waiting for the destruction. Suddenly, she realized that something was wrong. "Cease fire! Cease fire! CEASE FIRE!" she thundered. But it was too late. The blue beam that emanated from the Drej mothership began to change from an ice blue to a warm color. Positive energy was flowing from the *Titan* back into the Drej mothership! The queen Drej watched in disbelief as bolts of electrical energy traveled through the walls and floor. She howled as the energy began to destroy her. Seconds later, in a swirling vortex of red energy, the mothership was destroyed, imploding, and finally disappearing down the shaft of the red energy beam like water rushing down a drainpipe. Within seconds there was no evidence that the Drej had ever existed.

In the next moment, the sides of the *Titan* burst open. Bright gravity beams gushed forth like huge beams of sunlight. Gaseous and liquid matter began to spin, forming a core. Slowly, it began to grow, collecting solid matter, gas, and ice crystals. It started to become sphere shaped, forming a molten solid mass. Clouds gathered at its surface as it grew, and tiny lightning flashes and bolts appeared. Amazingly, a new world was forming.

Cale and Akima stood on a cliff, staring in wonder at the newly created landscape. A soft, warm rain was falling down upon them, and warm rays of light began to stream from the heavens.

"This is *amazing*," said Akima in a reverent tone.

"I know," said Cale softly.

Akima turned to Cale. She had a serious question to ask. "What are you going to call it?" she wondered.

Cale thought for a moment. "I think I'll call it…Bob."

"Bob?" said Akima incredulously.

"You don't like Bob?" said Cale.

"You can't call a planet *Bob*!" she protested.

"Oh, so now you're the boss," said Cale in a mocking tone. "You're the king of Bob."

"Well, *no* but…" began Akima.

"What?" said Cale.

Akima looked into his eyes. "Can't you just call it Earth?" she finished.

Cale put both hands on her face. "Well no one said you had to live on Bob," he teased.

Akima smiled. "I'm…never…calling…it…that," she said slowly.

They drew closer, about to kiss. Suddenly, a familiar roar interrupted them. It was the *Valkyrie*, the ship that had brought them together. They looked up to see it rocket past. Stith and Gune waved at the pair from the bridge, Gune giggling wildly.

With their arms around each other, Cale and Akima waved back to their friends. They stood on the surface of a brand-new world, a brand-new planet, a brand-new home— a brand-new Earth.